Cupid

and

Psych

ĀNDIE M. LŎNG

CONTENTS

Cover by Tammy Clarke at The Graphics Shed. Photo from Adobe Stock.

This book is dedicated to Den.
He puts up with a lot.
Blame Cupid.

CHAPTER 1

Samara

"You're back!"

I was only half listening to my friend as Ebony took the seat beside me in Jax's coffee shop. I was too distracted, thinking about all the different ways me and my husband Johnny had made up for the weeks when he'd been a Whippet and when we'd had to spend time apart—it was a long story.

"I am. Did you miss me?" I beamed at my friend.

A crease formed between her brows. "I said, 'you need to watch your back'. One part of your journey to your best life has occurred, but there are still hurdles to jump until you arrive at your final destination."

Ebony was a seer, and always coming out with

random statements that 90% of the time she couldn't back up with any advice that was actually helpful.

"Cheers, Ebs. I'll bear that in mind. As long as Johnny isn't having to jump the hurdles, we'll be okay."

"It's Greyhounds who race, not Whippets, dahling."

I stuck out my tongue. "Not true. They do Whippet racing in Yorkshire, so there."

She shook her head slowly. "You need to get out more. Although that's not in your future either." An evil smirk lit up her face.

"Ebony Marsden. Explain that comment." My voice got louder with each word.

"From fucked to fucked-up." She said, although in her cut-glass accent, it sounded like farked. Her eyes twinkled with amusement.

She refused to say anything else.

Freaking seers.

"So I was only gone a short while and yet Charlie got married and you got pregnant!" I said to Shelley. Shelley owned Withernsea Dating Agency and was going to be helping my friend, Max, get the 'Undate-ables' side of his Cupid service set up. Both Max and

I were on a trial probation. We'd re-graduated Cupid School and were now about to open a branch of Cupid Inc here in Withernsea. Today was Friday and one of my last days of freedom before work started on Monday.

"I know. I'm not supposed to get pregnant for another hundred years, but Fate decided I should get to experience a whole pregnancy at a normal rate." Her daughter Charlie had not only been an accelerated pregnancy, but had aged to her twenties within a year, as she had been prophesised, and now was, the Queen of Withernsea.

"What fun. Sickness, piles, and stretch marks. Good old Fate." I laughed.

Shelley rolled her eyes and Ebony sniggered.

"Well, we're really happy about it." Shelley beamed. "Anyway, when is Max getting here? I've spoken to him so much on the phone now. I can't wait to meet him in real life."

"Any minute and you're going to regret saying that." Max's confidence in himself was growing daily. He was calling Withernsea his fresh start and his chance to shine.

The coffee shop door opened, and Max came through it as if it were a stage curtain.

"Morning, bitches." He announced. Then he

threw a handful of unicorn coloured star confetti in front of him and passed through it. I'd told you he'd called it his chance to shine. He was sparkling with all the freaking glitter.

"And this is Max." I announced to their open-mouthed faces. "And you thought you'd seen everything in Withernsea. Tell Charlie her reign as queen is being threatened again." I told Shelley.

Max walked over and took everyone's palm in turn and kissed the back of their hand. Shelley, Ebony, and Jax were already in love with him, I could see it in their expressions. He *was* adorable. Rather like having a teacup dog dressed in a tutu; except today he'd left his at home. Speaking of pets, the door opened again, and Maisie came in. Maisie was a werecat.

"Could I have a saucer of milk please?" She asked Jax. Jax's head swivelled around to the empty counter.

"Where's my bloody employee gone now?" She groaned, getting up and going into the back.

"Trouble with the staff?" I asked Ebony.

"Bartholomew has a broken heart and Jax keeps finding him sobbing in the bathroom."

"Alyssa ditched him?" Alyssa was a werewolf who worked for Ebony in the boutique next door.

"Yup. She said she was focusing on herself for a while and didn't want to be tied down at such a young age."

Jax came out from the staff area with her arm around one of Bartholomew's ripped and bulging biceps. I focused my attention on Max's face.

"Oh my fuh-kkiinng god. Who is that walking throbbing member?"

I guffawed with laughter. "That, my friend, is our newly-single barista. But he's straight, sorry."

"Was straight if I get my way. Just my type. Big bushy beard and a groin that's gonna mean I can't walk for days."

"Quieten down." I told my overexcited friend.

"My daughter calls him Sir Loins." Shelley added. "Because she says he's a prime bit of beef."

"Oh, that is soooo his name from now on. Behind his back of course."

Max performed a dramatic hand flounce in the barista's direction. "Hey, Bart baby, could I get a skinny latte with soy milk? Thanks, boyfriend."

Bartholomew glared at Max, who raised both eyebrows.

"Easy, tiger. I can have real milk if it's a problem." Max looked at me. "Dramatic, or what?"

"No-one calls him Bart." I informed him. "Because his surname is Simpson."

"Well, a heads-up would have been nice, Samara, darling, don't you agree?" He sighed and then he swivelled his head, looking around the room. "Hey, where did that dark-haired woman go?"

I pointed to the corner where a black cat was enjoying a saucer of cat milk.

"The woman is a cat? Aaarrrggh." Max jumped onto his chair.

"What on earth is wrong with you now?" I rolled my eyes.

"You know my feelings on pussy." He said. Then he laughed loudly and sat back down.

"Sorry, I just had to do that." He turned to Shelley. "I'm not like this all the time, honey. I'm just so excited about being here."

I mimed behind his back. "All. Of. The. Time."

"So you're Rebecca's brother?" She asked him.

"For my sins, yes. Although she has to be nice now. Cupid's watching her with his new business being here. It has to be a success you see. Cupiding needs to find its new path. Speaking of the new business, have you found me my first undateable to work on yet?"

"I have." Shelley pointed to the cat. "You'll be working with Maisie. She's been on my books for a while now, and her dates never end well. We've had allergies. She stole one date's years supply of mackerel fillets from his pantry. The list of disasters is endless."

"You'd better give me this guy's details too. I'm guessing if he keeps a years supply of mackerel, he's not found his ideal partner either."

"Well, just start with Maisie, hey, first? See how you get on. She's quite a handful, and I don't mean when she's furry."

"Fabulous. Well, that's my first victim, I mean client. Now you just need yours." Max grinned at me.

"She has one." Ebony said.

"No, I don't." I protested.

"Believe me, you do. Just go to work on Monday morning and your client will arrive."

"Anyone I know?"

"Yes, you know them."

"Who is it?"

Ebony looked at her watch. "Oh is that the time? I'd better return to my boutique." She turned to Jax. "Make sure he doesn't serenade Alyssa today please. It was off-putting to the customers." She turned to me. "I'll see you Sunday at the grand opening of your new venture."

"Ooh, you're coming? Great."

She covered her mouth with her hand and tittered. "I wouldn't miss it for the world."

After enjoying a catch up with my friends, I walked down to the next block where my pet grooming parlour was, 'Short Bark and Sides'. I did groom any pets booked in by prior appointment, but the business was mainly dog grooming, and the local werewolf pack who were too hairy for a normal barber.

While I'd been away in London, a lady called India had been brought in by Cupid Inc to look after the place. Luckily for me, she had agreed to stay on. A tall, slim brunette, it was clear to see she enjoyed working with animals. She was a shy, introverted woman who I'd yet to persuade to go and meet everyone at the coffee shop.

I pushed open the door and saw India was in the washroom with a pampered Pekingese. I stood in the washroom doorway. "Everything been okay?"

"Yes, thank you. No problems at all. I've taken a couple of extra bookings for next week too."

My parlour only opened part-time around the

bookings. We tried to book in over just three days of a week but could do more if necessary. I'd needed a flexible job to work around Cupiding, although of late I'd not done too much of that. India appeared laid back and happy to do whatever was needed. She struck me as one of those meditative types who did regular yoga and chanted. She smelled like Patchouli oil when she wasn't smelling like dog shampoo.

"I've been down to the coffee shop. They are still asking when you're going to pop in."

"Oh, I will one day. I'm not a coffee drinker though. Do they do Matcha?"

"Hmm, not sure. I'll ask Jax. That building's better known for matchmaking than matcha, so watch out if you're single. Ebony will be telling you who you're destined for and Shelley will try to get you on the books."

Her eyes widened.

"And that's why you don't want to go in." I realised.

"I'm sure they are lovely people. I've said hello to them in passing, but I really like my quiet life and I hate people trying to matchmake me. My parents were like it all the time at home, 'come and meet whoever's son'. I'll find my love when destiny decides."

I shivered at the word destiny. That was the name the woman who had recently tried to poison me had assumed, though she was really called Janine.

"It's Fate actually who usually decides. I've met her. Hopefully she's finished with me and she can start on you now."

India put more shampoo on the Pekingese and began massaging it in. "Withernsea is full of very strange people. I'm a human and I much prefer animals to be honest with you. They're much less complicated."

Not when your husband's a Whippet, I wanted to add, but I kept my mouth shut. I didn't want her thinking every client was a human or supe in disguise. She had to take Rescue Remedy to shave the weres as it was.

"Will you come to the opening of Cupid Inc tomorrow if I promise to look after you and not let any of my friends accost you? You really could do with introducing yourself to the locals. It might drum up some extra business."

She bit her lip. "Okay. Just for a small part of it; but if it gets too much for me, I will have to leave."

"That's my girl." I beamed. The dog grinned at

me showing its teeth, thinking the praise was for itself.

"Did you think I meant you, gorgeous pooch? Did you?"

The dog shook its body, furiously splashing soap suds all over. Mainly, I'd also take a pet over a human any day. Except my husband, although he'd been cute as a fawn-coloured Whippet. However, he was even cuter as a fair-haired love god. I checked the time on the wall clock.

Ooh, he'd be home from work soon. Time to get home and get into bed naked ready to welcome him.

Life was good right now, with no picky parents around and no one trying to harm me. I had my fabulous husband back, a new career, a booming business that I only had to manage now, and my amazing friends around me.

"Thanks, Fate." I muttered in case she could hear me. "And if you're not busy, India might need a helping hand."

CHAPTER 2

Fate

*U*sually I wouldn't have picked up on Samara's murmurings as I'd have moved on, but of course my plans for her were not finished. She needn't have worried; India was already in my sights and she was going to surprise them all.

But now I just needed to wait until the little surprise I had for Samara made itself known. I was sure it wouldn't be much longer...

CHAPTER 3

Jessica

There were two one-bedroomed apartments above the new Cupid Inc building, and I'd taken one, Max the other. I stood outside my car in the car park behind the new Cupid Inc premises. It was packed to the roof with my belongings. Here was my home and my employment for the foreseeable future. The truth was, I was excited to start something new. Yes, I would miss counselling the students at Cupid School, but I expected this new role would be a lot more interesting... and a lot further away from my ex-husband.

Leaving everything in the car for now, I walked to the back entrance and unlocked the door that housed the staircase leading up to my new home.

The inside smelled of fresh paint and newly laid carpet and I breathed it in.

New beginnings.

I was a psychologist and was here to assist my friends Samara and Max with their new ventures for Cupid Inc. It was important these probation periods were a success as Cupid would then roll the businesses out elsewhere.

I had Cupid on speed dial given he was my ex-father-in-law.

It was the big secret no one could know about.

A divorce in Cupid's direct family line.

An embarrassment of the family name.

He could take that right to the door of his son. He was the one who put his career first and stopped giving a damn about us. Anyway, new beginnings, I reminded myself, unlocking the door.

The apartment was furnished in creams and taupe's and given I was only paying a nominal rent; it was exquisitely decorated. I should have known my ex-father-in-law wouldn't just give me the basics. I flopped down onto the sumptuous black couch which moulded to my body and I laid back and sighed.

The truth was, I wasn't over my ex.

I wasn't sure I ever would be.

But you couldn't make someone love you if they didn't want to.

Shaking myself from my stupor, I made myself get back up and check out the rest of the place and then I started the process of bringing my belongings into my new home.

"Hey, roomie!" Max shouted through my partially opened doorway.

I smiled at him. "Come on in."

He walked through looking around. "Very nice." He said, "My walls are purple. They know me so well."

He took a seat on the sofa without being asked. "You should have come to Jax's. They're a great crowd. How lucky that they get to hang there every day. It's a little too far from us here."

"We can buy Jax's blend and we have a coffee pot in the office." I reassured him. "Also there's an ice-cream parlour a few doors down called Jetty's, and next door to that is a sandwich shop with seating called 'Tasty Bites' which apparently is new."

"Really? Oh my." Max patted his stomach.

"We're in trouble, fella. Big trouble. So how do you know all this? You only just got here."

"I procrastinated unpacking for over an hour and walked down the street. Then of course, the arcade around the corner sells chips and waffles."

Max took out his mobile and furiously pressed his keypad. "That's my reminder for in three months to book in for a gastric band."

I smiled. "So are you all unpacked then?"

"If unpacked is having thrown all my belongings in the living room then yes I've unpacked." He shrugged. "I'll just unpack as I need things. I met Shelley, she's so lovely. Oh and I have my first victim already."

"Will you stop calling them that. You're going to be saying it to their face." I shook my head at him. "Now give me the details."

"She's called Maisie and she's a werecat. Pretty thing. Black."

"I thought you didn't rate women, and also watch out commenting on skin colour; it shouldn't be relevant."

He threw his head back on the sofa and emited a dramatic sigh. "I meant she was a pretty black cat."

"Oh."

"Anyway, that weird friend of Sam's was there—

Ebony—and she said Sam's first client will arrive Monday, straight delivered to the branch, so we're up and running, baby." He raised a hand to smack against mine and then dropped it when I failed to meet it, given I was standing three feet away and not walking over just to high-five him.

"You let me hang." He shook his head. "I can't believe you let me hang."

"I'm letting you hang out here. That should be enough for you. Don't think you're spending all your spare time here either. I don't have time to keep vacuuming up that unicorn confetti that's dropping out of your pocket. I'm guessing you wanted to make an entrance this morning?"

"Of course. They need to remember the first time they met me."

"Oh I don't think there's any danger of them forgetting." I mumbled under my breath.

Max went to his phone again and tapped keys. "So, girlfriend, to make sure our schedules align. Tomorrow, it's all about getting the building ready for the grand opening on Sunday, takeaway at yours, and then Monday 8am, we open the doors of Cupid Inc."

"Pedal back there, fella. Takeaway at mine?"

"Don't mind if I do." He spread his hand over his

chest. "Oh I'm so happy you live next-door. It's going to be am-ayyy-zzing. Right, got to dash. I have a back, sack, and crack scheduled. Got to look my best for Sunday."

Oh my god, I hoped he wasn't still thinking of doing a naked conga down to the beach to go skinny dipping.

My first night in my new apartment passed peacefully. The mattress was memory foam and my sleep undisturbed. After a shower, coffee, and a slice of toast, I grabbed my bag and made my way down the stairs and around to the front of the building. There was an access door at the bottom of the stairwell for Max and me to use, but I wanted to stare at the outside of my new place of work.

I stood stock still at the front of the building. It looked like Cupid and Christmas had a baby.

How had they done this by 10am?

The outside of the building was festooned with pink and silver Cupids and angels. The large window of Cupid Inc that faced the reception—which the last time I'd visited had a venetian blind covering it—now was uncovered and a white Christmas tree blocked most of the window. It also was decorated in pink and silver with huge swathes of what I presumed were tinsel but could easily pass for feather boas. A pink carpet went from the entrance to the front of the property.

"She's here. What do you think?" Max beamed.

"It's very…"

"Pink? Over-the-top? Dramatic? Migraine inducing? That's what I've come up with so far," said Rebecca, Max's sister. She rolled her eyes at him.

"Oh shut up, Miss Pissy Pants. Just because I got my own way for once. Slither back to where you came from if you don't like it."

Max and his sister did not get along. Then again, most people found Rebecca difficult to stomach seeing as she loved to be number one and was forever attention seeking. If I ever met their parents I would hug them hard. They must have thrown a party when they both left, that or slept for a year solid.

"Where's Samara?"

"The lazy sod has fallen asleep on the couch in your counselling room." Max said. "I reckon she had another wild night with the husband with how tired and pale she looked this morning. She needs to see daylight; she's spending far too much time in nocturnal pursuits."

I sighed. It had been a long, long time since I'd

gotten any that wasn't provided by something with batteries.

"I know that face." Max walked over and hugged me to his chest. "Because I wear it myself and so does poo-face over there. It's the look of the single person. We need to get laid. How does it look that we work for Cupid and we're single? We need to practice what we preach, so all three of us need a date asap. Agreed?"

"Do not be trying to matchmake me, brother."

"Why not? I'm in charge of the undateables now. You're perfect."

"Fuck off."

"I'm going to make a coffee. Then you can tell me what I need to do to help here." I began to walk towards the staff room.

"Throw all this out and start again." I heard Rebecca tell Max.

"Throw you out and start again." Max chuntered back.

Thank goodness my office was soundproofed for confidentiality.

After I'd made myself a drink, I pushed the door to my office open and watched as Samara opened one eye, paused with a confused look on her face, and then slowly sat up, pushing her curly blonde hair out of her face.

"What happened?"

"Apparently, you fell asleep in here."

"I came in to open your blind and then my eyes were just closing. Couldn't resist a little lie down."

"Well maybe you should sleep at night?" I winked.

"I did, I promise. I wasn't feeling too good, so I actually went to bed early."

"Well, looks like your body is playing catch up. Anyway, if you want to wake up fast just go and look at the pretty decorations, because Christmas and Valentine's made a baby outside."

"Oh God. I told him to take what he wanted to do and hold back three-quarters of it."

"Then I dread to think what he had planned. It looks like a Barbie dream home. A pink paradise."

Samara slowly edged herself off the couch, walked over to me, took the drink from my hand and threw it down her throat like a chaser.

"I'm off to kick some arse." She said.

"Rebecca's out there."

"Even better."

Rebecca and Samara were currently having to

work on their professional relationship. Having worked as Cupid representatives in neighbouring districts, there had been no love lost between the two of them. Cupid had had enough and was making them work as a team to get past it. They were civil, but it was clear to see that they actually wanted to punch each other in the throat. I didn't know about therapy sessions for clients, I think the staff needed help first, especially Rebecca. She was at the centre of two lots of conflict, one with her brother and one with Samara. I wondered if there was anyone she actually got along with.

Samara dragged the Christmas tree to the corner of the reception and put the blind back down but open.

Max opened his mouth to protest, but Samara just stood with her arms folded over her chest.

"Take up the pink fake-leopard skin rug off the floor and go burn it. And if one piece of unicorn confetti comes out today, I'll add you to the pyre."

An hour later the place was still decorated with pink and silver but at least now it was relatively toned down. A table had been placed in the reception ready for a buffet that Jax was catering, and Samara had set up a display on the reception counter of leaflets detailing our services.

"I don't think it's appropriate for you to display business cards and price lists for your grooming parlour here. It should be Cupid Inc stuff only." Rebecca huffed.

Samara looked ready to bludgeon Rebecca to death with the box the leaflets had come out of.

"Maybe for the opening it should just be Cupid Inc stuff, but let's get a noticeboard and a leaflet holder and encourage the community to share their offerings here. After all, they're all places for people to meet which is what we're all about isn't it?" I said.

"Fine." Samara harrumphed.

Rebecca looked smug.

Samara addressed her directly. "By the way, Rebecca. You must have sat in some chocolate before you came here. At least I hope it's chocolate. You have a huge patch of something brown on your butt cheek. Please don't sit on any of the furniture. We don't want it looking shitty."

Rebecca shot off in the direction of the bathroom.

"There's nothing on her backside is there?" I queried.

"Nope, but she is a shit and an arse so that is what she'll see in the mirror."

"Well, I've had all the fun I can handle for one day. I'll see you all tomorrow when we officially open this place."

That actually brought a big beaming smile to Samara's face. Then Max came into the room, and so did an annoyed looking Rebecca.

Samara held up a hand, went behind the reception counter and placed four champagne glasses and a bottle of fizz on the counter.

She popped the cork which hit Rebecca in one of her boobs.

"Sorry."

"It's fine. It's the most action that breast has seen in a long time." Rebecca quipped, shocking us all.

We burst out laughing and Samara poured and handed everyone a drink.

"To Cupid Inc." She said.

"To Cupid Inc." We toasted.

Then Samara's phone began ringing. She placed her drink down.

"Why? Did she do something to it? Freaking hell, Ebony, you drive me crazy."

She put the phone down.

"Everything okay?"

"She told me not to drink the champagne but won't say why, so everyone put it down. Talk about making the occasion fall flat."

"What did you do, buy a cheap bottle off the back of a van somewhere?" Rebecca quipped.

I left them to a new round of arguing. Surely, things could only get better?

CHAPTER 4

Samara

The one time I was running late and miserable because I had a bug and felt nauseous, would be the day I needed to be punctual and my usual bouncy and perky self.

I couldn't face breakfast and was putting Touche Eclat on my face like cement.

"They won't believe I'm late because I'm ill. They'll think we were shagging." I complained to Johnny.

He shrugged his shoulders. "Can't be helped that they think you can't resist me." He turned around and shook his arse at me.

"I can't resist you usually. Stupid bloody viruses getting in the way of my libido."

"I'm still willing to give you one even with your head in a bucket. You only have to ask."

"Ha ha."

"Okay, are you nearly ready? Because didn't you say the ribbon snipping was at eleven? It's half-past ten."

I groaned as my stomach rumbled. "I was supposed to be there for half-past nine. Rebecca will be jumping up and down in her eagerness to deliver some opinion on it."

Johnny grabbed my shoulders and stared down at me. "Stop focusing on that woman. I feel like there are three of us in this relationship. She's winning while she's winding you up, love. As Ella from Frozen says wisely, 'Let it go.'" He starts singing which reminded me of when he howled at the television when he was a Whippet and *For the Love of Dogs* came on.

"Fine. Come on then, let's get this show on the road." I told him and we headed towards Johnny's car.

Johnny's beeper went off, indicating an emergency at his veterinary surgery. He phoned in while I got myself comfy in the passenger seat. I could just go back to sleep. My eyes were closing when Johnny spoke. "Oh dear. Sorry, I'll drop you off, but then I'll have to go shoot down to the surgery. There's an emergency."

"It's fine. It's only a boring speech and a lame buffet. The animals need you more."

"I'll try to get back."

"Seriously, don't worry about it. I'm sure you won't miss anything important." I told him.

I really should learn not to tempt Fate. That woman had it in for me.

Cupid had come to open the building and to make a speech. Of course, most humans just thought it was hilarious that a man was pretending to be Cupid himself, not believing for a moment that he was the genuine article. I looked around the reception at the people milling around, recognising a few faces. India was right at the back hiding behind the Christmas tree. I waved and went over.

"Sorry, India. I've got a bit of a bug, so I'm running late. How are you doing?"

"I'm okay. To be honest I've only just come inside. There was a cat hanging about outside. Lovely little black thing. Dead fussy, so I've spent most of my time with that."

I didn't bother telling her that it was probably

Maisie, who was currently in human form and getting ever closer to the tuna sandwiches and party sausages on the buffet table.

"Right, well, if you'll excuse me a moment, I just need to let Max and Cupid know I'm here and then I'll come back over." She nodded and I went off in search of my colleagues and boss.

"Glad you could make it." Rebecca drawled in a tone that told me she'd hoped I'd miss the event altogether.

"I'm so sorry, Cupid." I said to my boss. "I have a stomach flu."

"Well you're here to listen to my amazing speech so no harm done. Hopefully it's a twenty-four-hour thing so you can get off to an efficient start tomorrow."

"Oh yes. I can't wait to start reviewing Rebecca's past records to see if there are any mistakes I need to rectify." I smiled at her sweetly. "Sorry, I mean anyone in need of aftercare." Although we had background checks to do as Cupids, for most that was it before they 'pointed and shot' their arrows. Rebecca was a point and shooter, p&s for short. I preferred to check up on those I'd matched to see if the match was successful, or if not, to see if there was anything I could do. I called this aftercare and that was what my new probation period was focusing on. Rebecca would ensure she p&s'd enough people, both in Withernsea and neighbouring Hornsea-which I'm sure she would because she certainly p&s'd me and Max off-and I would focus on a couple of cases of aftercare, including going back over Rebecca's last couple of years of Cupiding.

"If only I'd also been given the power to shoot friendship arrows." Cupid shook his head and walked over to the microphone we'd had erected at the side of the reception area.

"If I could have everyone's attention please." He asked. "Then once I get my speech done, we can enjoy the lovely buffet."

I knew then that his speech wasn't going to be long. Nothing got in the way of Cupid and food.

"Today marks an important day in my life as Cupid. A new way of working where we embrace the modern life. With the advent of dating agencies and apps, Cupid has needed to rethink a few things, and this is the first of those. A place where people who find it difficult to get anyone to date them for any period of time can come; and a place where those who were matched but who still have feelings for each other can see if Cupid and counselling can work together to heal any cracks in the relationship.

"Of course, we still need to make sure enough people around the world are matchmade, and for that we also have a Point & Shooter in the team. So I'd like to ask—and I'm saying them in alphabetical order, because they're a prickly bunch even without arrows—Max, Rebecca, and Samara, please step forward."

We all walked alongside Cupid.

"So firstly, introducing Max who will be working alongside those struggling to date; Rebecca, who will keep uniting matches; and Samara, who will be ensuring those couples that still have love stay together." He looked around the room. "Ah, Jessica, please step forward."

Jessica came and stood at my side. "I hate this." She whispered.

"Jessica is our psychologist who will be assisting our Cupid representatives where needed. This is my fantastic team, and so without further ado I will cut the ribbon currently stopping access to the buffet and declare this building open." He snipped the ribbon, and everyone burst into a round of applause.

"Enjoy your five minutes of fame because I intend to be the best Cupid rep around Withernsea, honey." Rebecca whispered close to my ear. It was at that moment that the smell of the tuna sandwiches hit my nostrils and a vomit tsunami rolled through me.

I threw up all over Rebecca's legs and shoes.

Well, Johnny had told me to let it go...

Rebecca gave out a blood curdling scream and started heaving. "Oh my god, oh my god. There's puke on my legs and my shoes." A middle-aged woman with curly, honey-blonde hair came running forwards with a massive pile of paper towels and started dabbing at Rebecca's feet. "I'm Mabel, lovie, the domestic. I'll have you cleaned up in a jiffy."

Jessica led me to her office and got me to lie down on that gorgeous couch. "Oh, Samara. Maybe you should have stayed at home?" She took a bottle of water out of a mini-fridge in the room, unfastened it and passed it to me. I sat up and took a sip, enjoying the cool freshness on my tongue.

"I feel fine now. In fact, I could do with some-thing to eat. I'm just tired, which for me is entirely normal."

Jessica's eyes narrowed and she looked at me in an appraising way I didn't like.

"Samara?"

"Yes?"

"Is there any chance you could be pregnant?"

I guffawed. "Oh god, no way. No, Johnny and I use contraception. It's firmly wrapped and I don't take the packaging off that present. There are some gifts you don't want to receive."

"They're not foolproof, but fair enough, if you use protection maybe it is a stomach bug. It's just a friend of mine used to do that puking and then wanting to eat thing. Plus, you've always had a great rack, but your boobs look super-perky and full."

I looked down. They did seem a teeny bit bigger. I ran my past shagging Olympics through my mind and then my life came to a crashing, stomach-churning halt. My face must have told the story as Jessica's wastepaper basket was held beneath my chin as I chundered once more.

"When Johnny was turned back into a human. We didn't think..." I stared at Jessica. "I shagged Johnny without a johnny. The irony. I can't be pregnant. I don't want one." I could feel my breath coming in shorter gasps as I clutched for air. "Is this room getting smaller, the walls? They're closing in. Oh my."

It went dark.

When I came to, Jessica was at the side of me on the couch and my feet were elevated.

Everything came flooding back.

Was I pregnant?

As my gasping started again, Jessica passed me a brown paper bag. "Breathe into it, Samara, and calm down. You might not be. We need to get you a test so you can find out one way or another."

A knock came at the door.

"Let me go and see who that is."

I nodded, incapable of doing anything else.

Shelley's voice was recognisable from the crack in the door. "Come in, Shelley. Actually, you might be able to help."

Shelley's brow was creased as she walked towards me. "Hey, lovely. How are you feeling? I thought I'd come to check because you've been in here a while."

I removed the brown paper bag. "It's possible..." My breath quickened. "I might..."

Shelley spoke an incantation and smoke-like tendrils swirled from her fingers, wrapping around me and making me feel calmer. My breath calmed to a stage where I could speak again. It really benefited to have a part-witch, part-vampire as a friend.

"That is a seriously good trick and I might need it for the foreseeable if shit has hit the fan."

Shelley looked from me to Jessica and back again. "What's going on?"

"I'm wondering if I might be pregnant, and you know my feelings on babies after how I was brought up."

"Well, you are not your parents, but let's save that conversation for later. Luckily you have a super-speedy part-vampire at your disposal. Give me a mo." And with that the only sign she'd gone was the whoosh of the door and my hair blowing a little.

In no time at all she was back. She pointed to the bathroom off the counselling room. "Off you go."

I followed the instructions from the box, my hands shaking the whole time I did it. I placed the test on the side and waited for the longest minutes in history.

But before they could appear my phone buzzed in my pocket.

Ebs: Thanks for the entertainment and congrats!

Was she saying...?

I looked over at the plastic. It was a digital test and so I couldn't say I was confused by the result when it appeared on the screen.

PREGNANT

I swallowed. My worst fears had come to life. The responsibility of a baby. What if I screwed its life up? How the hell could I look after a child? I could barely look after myself.

There was no question about not keeping it though. I thought of a baby looking like a miniature version of my husband and my heart fluttered a little.

Could I do this?

Could I be a mum?

One thing I knew for sure. Its maternal grandparents weren't getting anywhere near it.

And that's when it all clicked into place. Because powerful feelings of over-protectiveness came out of nowhere. A dogged determination to keep fuckers like my evil parents away and to love it with a love I'd never got to experience from my own.

All this overwhelming emotion and I'd only been pregnant for approximately one-and-a-half minutes.

CHAPTER
5

Jessica

"*D*o you think I should have gone in with her in case she fainted again?" Shelley asked.

I shook my head.

"No, she needs to do this on her own. If the test is positive, she might need a moment. If she wants us, she'll call out. Either that or we'll hear the thud as she hits the floor in a faint."

"Well, if it's positive and she's in shock, I can sympathise." Shelley rubbed her stomach. "I'm thirteen weeks pregnant and seeing as I wasn't supposed to be able to get pregnant again for another hundred years, this one kind of took me by surprise."

"Oh congratulations." I said, while I processed the hundred years bit. I knew about supernaturals but being up close and personal with them in Withernsea would take some getting used to.

"Thanks."

"Maybe you're best placed to give her some advice then if she comes out of the bathroom saying she's pregnant."

"I'll try, depending on the level of hysteria."

We smiled at each other.

Then the bathroom door opened, and Samara walked out, but rather than hysterical she seemed serene but tearful. "I'm having a baby." She said. "And I already love it. What the fuck is happening to me?"

She burst into noisy tears and Shelley grabbed her shoulders and gave her a huge hug.

Another knock at the door had me rolling my eyes. Who now?

The door opened and Kim walked through. Kim worked with Shelley at the dating agency and was married to a werewolf, Darius. I'd been told she had three werebabies when I'd met her earlier. Or as she'd put it, 'thank fuck for having this opening ceremony. I've left the trio of brats with daddy, auntie, and granny and legged it here to support a fellow business. Now where's the wine?'

"Are you having a private party in here and forgot to invite me?" She spotted Samara who was sat on the couch crying. "What's up with her? They discontinued her favourite lipstick?"

Samara turned to Kim, her lips trembling.

"I'm p-pregnant."

"Yeah? Cry about it if you find out you're having three. Otherwise, get a grip."

"*Kim,*" Shelley admonished. "She's in shock."

"Yeah, so was my vajayjay when I birthed three cubs."

"Well, this isn't about you. It's about me." Samara wiped her eyes and pouted in Kim's direction.

"And there she is. Congrats, Sam. You're going to be a mummy. Welcome to the club."

Shelley looked over to me and raised a brow. "Who knew a small room like this could fit in two diva personalities."

Kim took a seat next to Samara. "So, how ya feeling?"

"I thought I'd be hysterical with fright, but I just feel really overprotective, like if anyone tries to upset them ever, I'll kill them."

"Ah, see, your motherly instinct has already kicked in." Kim hugged her. "You need to get yourself fixed up and go tell that husband of yours he's going to be a daddy."

Shelley turned to me. "Wait until they have teenagers. My daughter was only one for part of a year, but I'd have sold her given half a chance."

They all said their goodbyes and left over the next few minutes and then I found myself alone in my office. All the three women had bonded over the fruits of their womb and there I was childless and alone. I sat back on my own couch as memories hit and I found myself powerless to stop them.

I was late. Two days late. We'd been trying for over six months and I'd started to wonder if there was a problem, but my breasts were so painful I couldn't remove my bra and something inside me told me that this time it had happened.

Lachlan got up to hit the shower, and he banged on the bathroom door.

"Jess, come on. I need to get to work, I'm leading an important case."

I sighed and pulled up my panties. When wasn't he? He spent more and more time at work, telling me he was trying to get himself a promotion to Sergeant, but I'd been hearing this for over a year now and nothing had changed. Actually, that wasn't true. Lachlan had changed, being out for hours. Not only was he in the police, he was the son of Cupid and so also had to matchmake regularly. It was in his genes. Had I known this when I'd met him, I'd have walked away, but unfortunately, I'd fallen hook, line, and sinker before he'd revealed the truth about his parentage.

I walked out of the bathroom. "Hey, good news, I thin-"

"Tonight, Jess, okay. I'm running really late now. You can get showered anytime this week, can't you? It is the holidays, right?"

I was training to be a psychologist and he was right; we were currently on leave. At least he'd paid attention to that. I didn't think he'd even looked me in the eyes yet this morning.

I walked past him out of the bathroom, feeling like a ghost in my own home.

That morning, I went to the supermarket and bought a test. Then I sat in my bathroom and held my breath at times while I waited for the result. When the line appeared in the box, I was beside myself with emotion. I was pregnant. Finally, I was pregnant. I *spent the day clutching my tummy, joining Mumsnet and BabyCentre. I went out and bought a pregnancy magazine and a pair of white booties that I planned to put on Lachlan's dinner plate that evening.*

But the dinner went cold with no sign of my husband.

As I went to bed, I realised I'd got a text.

Lachlan: Don't wait up. We have a lead.

The other side of my bed was still empty the next morning. I checked my phone.

Lachlan: Sorry can't call. Delicate situation. I'm going to stay down here. Got a hotel room so I can be where needed.

Where he needed to be was here, but he wasn't.

Later that afternoon, I went to the bathroom and

found I was bleeding. The doctors said it could have been an early miscarriage or a false positive result. Whichever, I felt a loss so immense I thought I would die. And there was no one there to share this with me, certainly not my husband.

When he finally returned home, I'd burned the magazine and the bootees.

We sat at dinner and he said. 'I think I did it. This is going to have got me that promotion'. He never asked me what my own news had been. Maybe he didn't care. But I knew then that I was done.

"I want a divorce. I'm leaving you." I told him.

His face had drained of all colour. Now he knew how I felt. He begged me to change my mind, but something inside me had hardened and I felt distant and impossible to reach.

I left and didn't look back.

Standing up straight and composing myself, I closed the door on my office and my thoughts, and I made my way back out to the opening ceremony. It was time for my life to move forward and who knew? With a dating agency on my doorstep and three Cupids at my disposal, maybe my own new time for love might be right around the corner?

CHAPTER 6

Samara

*J*ohnny came home thoroughly overexcited.

"Wife, strip and wait for me in the bedroom because do you know who you're married to?" He shouted from the doorway.

I walked into the hall and leaned against the doorframe.

"Tom Hardy?"

"Tom Hardy is nothing special at the side of this guy here." He pointed a finger at himself. "I just saved the life of a cat... and her six little kittens."

"Oh my god. You amazing man. We'll have to call you the Pussy Master."

"I already had that title. Let's add Supervet to the mix."

I shook my head. "Nope, I love you, but you're no match for Noel 'Supervet' Fitzpatrick."

"Damn television guy with his fiendish skills. Are we sure he's not supernatural? The guy stays up half the night to operate too. I smell a rat."

"That'll be what the cat had for tea."

He laughed. "Why are you still in the doorway and not naked in our bedroom?"

"Because." I swallowed. "I have some news of my own. You might want to come and sit down."

He pursed his lips. "The last time this happened you just wanted to tell me Kylie Jenner had brought out a new shade of gloss."

"I promise this time it's bigger than that and sitting down worthy."

He began to move past me, shaking off his shoes and moving into the living room. "A new series of Love Island has been announced?"

"No."

"Joe Browns have a sale on, and you've spent a grand?"

"I wouldn't confess to a Joe Brown sale if there was. Now shut up and *sit down*."

He plonked himself down on the sofa and I sat opposite him.

"Before you tell me your news, I've got to get this

out there. I really want one of the kittens. They're so cute and there's this gorgeous black one that has just a white patch over one eye."

"Johnny, for heaven's sake."

"I know, I know, but hear me out. We said we'd get a pet to ease us into there being three of us, and a cat would be perfect because they're self-reliant to a large degree, and if it gets ill, I can care for it and-"

"I'm pregnant. We're having a baby, Johnny."

There was a large silence. Mainly because my husband's mouth was gaping open.

He then actually shook his head as if there was something that had got in his ears and he needed it to come out. It reminded me of when he'd been a Whippet post-bath.

"Say that again. I can't have heard right."

"I'll tell you a story, Johnny. Once upon a time there was a man who'd been turned into a Whippet by Fate. She turned him back and he had sex multiple times with his wife without the use of contraception, such was their joy at being reunited. Fate decided it was time for them to have a baby and so now the wife is pregnant. The end."

A huge boom sounded in the flat and a woman with blue and black hair appeared in the living room.

"Talk of the Devil." I huffed.

"I'm not Satan, Samara, as you well know. I am Fate. I just wanted to confirm that you are indeed with child. Your baby is due around the seventh of July."

"Thank you for that nugget of information. Now there comes a time in a woman's life when she has some special exciting news for her husband, such as news of their first child. Then they probably hug and kiss with joy. Or, it could be like my living room where a stupified husband sits on the sofa and Fate herself turns up unannounced and stands in the middle of the happy couple."

"Oh, er, yes. I see. Well, congrats. Bye."

Boom.

"Seriously, that woman."

"Yeah, but she's gone now." Johnny winked, looking much more his usual self. He stood up and stalked towards me. A frisson of excitement pulsed in my core. He'd got that horny look about him.

"Well, wife. What a day. Not only have I proved my excellence in the surgery, but I come home, and my prowess is proved by the fact I have put a bun in your oven. I'm on fire. So, get into the bedroom Baby Mama because I want to dip my wick."

He wrapped his arms around me and pulled me close, planting a huge kiss to my lips.

"Are you happy, Sam, about the baby? Given your own family history."

"I really am. Yes, it was a complete shock, but I can't wait to meet our little baby."

"So before I do carry you into our bedroom to do dastardly things to you, how did you find out?"

"Well," I smiled. "Firstly, I threw up down Rebecca, so this baby already has good taste."

He high-fived me. That's why I married this man. He just got me completely.

Then he picked me up and carried me into the bedroom.

We'd arranged to meet Max for Sunday dinner at The Marine, a pub near the beach front. They did an all-day carvery with a veggie option for Max. It was so cheap there was no point in cooking.

When Johnny and I arrived, we found him seated at a table with Rebecca and the domestic, Mabel.

I raised a brow.

"So, my sister decided to tag along, and I invited Mabel because she had no plans for the evening and I thought it would be a good bonding experience, though Jess blew us out."

"She got other plans?" I asked.

"Yeah, brooding in her apartment. I don't know what happened but when she came back out of the office after sorting you out after Pukefest, something was different. She just didn't seem herself."

"Hmmm, I'll ask her tomorrow. I hope I didn't upset her somehow. I don't remember doing anything."

"Like you ever do." Rebecca huffed under her breath. I let it go. I had puked on her earlier, plus I refused to let her spoil the day I found out I was pregnant.

"I'm surprised to see you here actually." Rebecca added. "I thought you'd be curled up in bed with how ill you were earlier."

I shook my head. "I feel amazing now. Must have passed off whatever it was." Johnny and I had decided there would be no announcements until I'd seen the doctor and had my early scan. I wanted to get to the docs as soon as possible so I'd be ringing first thing the next morning, to make it all official.

We ordered our meals and queued up for the lovely smelling food. I noticed India walk in, so I waved her over and invited her to join us.

The poor girl barely had time to take a bite of a roast potato before Max started on her.

"India, darling. I have my first client tomorrow to matchmake and well, she's a werecat. Any ideas on what kind of person might want to be matchmade with one of those? Any flaws about cats I should know about in particular, in order to avoid an error, only this one in particular is very erm..."

"Snobby, greedy, aloof, anyone's for a piece of fish." I filled in for him. "In other words, a regular kitty cat."

"Well, cats love to be warm, well fed, and able to be free to come and go as they please. They don't like being wet-"

Max interrupted, "I'm guessing you mean by water, rather than sexually?"

India went bright red.

"Max!"

"I need to make sure. It's important my first match goes very well."

"Oh yeah, you two are still on probation, unlike me." Rebecca's face was smug. A look I was realising she wore every chance she could. I couldn't wait to start going through her past caseload and turning her from smug to mug.

"So, India. Where did you live before Withernsea?" Max asked her.

"I'm from Hull but I've spent the last few years

travelling around. I find it hard settling down in one place."

"Been anywhere good?" Johnny asked.

"I did Australia and Thailand last year. Fabulous places."

"Withernsea must seem a bit of a come down after those." I added.

"Actually, I like it here. The place has an eclectic mix of people. I feel at home here. Like I finally found what I've been searching for."

"Well, I'm hoping for a place in the main team in London. That's where I want to be." Rebecca said. "Not stuck here for the rest of my days in Withernsea and Hornsea."

I realised then I'd got a quandary on my hands. I wanted to wipe the smug grin off her face but if she didn't succeed, I'd be stuck with her. If I wanted rid, then I had to kill Rebecca with kindness. Get her enough success that she was gone. Hmmm, food for thought indeed. My mind flipped through a few possible scenarios until I took a bite of roast beef and then all my thoughts were real food ones. I was so hungry, I flagged down the waitress and paid for another carvery dinner.

Returning to the table, four sets of eyes stared at me.

I shrugged. "I didn't get any lunch, did I?"

As I tucked into my second dinner, I noticed that Mabel, who'd sat at my left-hand side had a large white carrier bag on her lap. I'd thought it was a napkin until I'd given it a closer inspection.

She saw me notice it and whispered, "No one wants to see puke in a restaurant, love. So it's just in case you're," she coughs, "poorly again."

I smiled at her. "That's very kind of you to think of that. I need to be better prepared." I whispered back.

"I've got your back, love." She said. "Just until you're a bit further on."

My eyes began to swim with tears.

"Oh, love." She passed me a napkin. "That'll be the hormones. They'll be whooshing around at the min."

But as I dabbed at my eyes, I wanted to tell her she was wrong. It was just a virtual stranger had looked after me more than my own mother ever had.

"What's up with you?" Rebecca noticed me wiping my eyes.

"Bit my tongue." I lied.

"Could do with doing that a bit more often." She quipped.

I smiled at her and she looked at me disconcerted.

Yes, though it would kill me, Rebecca was going to be amazing at her job. So amazing she was on a one-way trip out of Withernsea.

CHAPTER
7

Jessica

That night I startled awake and watched as a breeze gusted through and blew my curtains into my room.

"What the...?"

I switched on the light so I could see more clearly and realised my window had been broken. There was a brick on the bedroom floor.

A banging at my door almost finished me off. I felt a cardiac arrest was imminent. Careful to not tread on any glass, I grabbed and slipped on my robe and checking through the spy hole, I opened the door to Max.

"What was that noise? Did you hear it? It sounded like a bomb. Do we need to evacuate?"

"Someone threw a brick through my window. It was probably kids messing around."

"At 2am? Won't they be in bed ready for school in the morning?"

I shrugged. "Well that's what it was anyway. A brick. I'd better find the number of a repair company."

"I've phoned the police."

I groaned. "Oh, Max. It's a broken window, not a murder. They won't care."

"Aren't you worried someone's like trying to threaten or hurt you or something?"

I yawned. I was too tired to give a shit. "It'd be far more likely that they'd want to get you, wouldn't it? Maybe they got the wrong flat and it's someone you matchmade in the past who has a grudge?"

His eyes went wide.

"Someone is trying to kill me, Jessica."

"Oh my god, Max. I'm winding you up. It's just kids." I held my hand up. "The kids who did this probably aren't planning on going to school tomorrow."

Yet another knock came. This time from the door at the bottom of the stairs. "I'll get it. It'll be the police." Max said and he disappeared from the room.

I just wanted to sleep. But now I had fresh air

whirling through the curtains, cooling my room to what felt like a Siberian temperature. It couldn't happen in summer. Oh no. It was 2:15am on the 3 December. I realised I'd now be facing the police in my pyjamas and robe and wished I had chance to get back dressed before they arrived. Walking through to the living room, I switched the central heating back on and put my gas fire on full. Then I filled the kettle because even if my guests didn't want a drink, I sure did.

The door pushed open and Max came through. "Are you decent, darling? It was the police."

"Sure, sweetie." I took the piss out of his greeting. "You can come in, I'm covered up."

Max walked through, turning to a man in the hallway. "So, like I said it was a brick that came through this gorgeous one's window. I must know that her life is not in danger, she's so very precious to me."

Dear God, get the man an Oscar for dramatic performance of the year.

I was about to tell him to calm down when the man behind him revealed himself.

Dark blonde hair, piercing blue eyes that seemed to speak to your soul, and lips that promised paradise.

"What are you doing here?" I addressed my ex-husband, pulling my robe tighter around myself.

"I transferred. I'm the new Sergeant in Withernsea." He told me. "More to the point, what are you doing here? It's rather a coincidence that we're in the same town."

"Your bloody father." I hissed. "I'm going to do him bodily harm."

Lachlan's eyes pierced through me. I watched as they appraised me, running over every inch of my skin. But though his gaze wasn't professional, he was.

"Well, I'll need to take a statement from you and look at the scene."

Max stood there agog for a moment before finding his voice. "Do you two know each other? You said about his father..."

He walked about like he was a detective.

"Oh my god, are you Jess' ex-husband?"

Lachlan nodded, though his gaze never left me.

"And you're working here in Withernsea? Oh my." He began to pace. "And it's too late to call Samara with this amazing gossip. I shan't sleep. I shan't." He walked back to Lachlan and held out his hand. "I'm Max. From tomorrow I work with your ex-wife at Cupid Inc. My job is to match the undate-ables. Your wife will assist if they need to talk issues through. I love your wife by the way. Ooops, I don't think you're supposed to tell a man you love their wife."

"Ex-wife." Lachlan enunciated slowly as if he wanted to punish me with each syllable as he shook Max's hand. "She divorced me."

Okay this was becoming even more awkward. "Max, it's way past your bedtime and we're up early tomorrow. Let me see you out."

Max pouted. "Just when it was getting good. Oh yeah, you'll keep me around while you're in potential danger, but ex-hubby turns up and it's bye, Max. Off you go."

I rolled my eyes and walked him to the door. "I'll tell you everything tomorrow okay? But only if you go straight to bed."

"Okay, honey bunny." He leaned over and kissed my cheek. "Love you bunches."

I closed the door and taking a deep inhale that I hoped might calm my racing heart a fraction, I walked back through to my apartment.

Lachlan was in my bedroom looking at the window and the brick. "I've called someone to come put a board up temporarily until you can get the window repaired tomorrow. They'll be here in thirty minutes."

"Do you want a drink? A coffee, maybe?"

"Why did you leave me, Jess?"

I stood stock still and then I turned. "Yes, I'll make some coffee." I walked out of the bedroom.

"I want a divorce. I'm leaving you." I told him.

Lachlan's face drained of all colour.

"Don't be crazy. I know I've been busy lately with work, but this promotion-"

"I don't care anymore, Lachlan. While you've been out there working on your career, I've been here realising that I've spent so much time without you that I don't need you anymore."

"You can't mean that."

"But I do. You have no idea what's happening in my life. In my world. None. You eat, sleep, and breathe that job and I may as well be a pillow on the bed. You make me feel like a ghost in my own home. Insubstantial. Like you can sense me, but you don't see me."

"It was just until this promotion was in the bag. You know this, we talked about it."

"You talked about it. I've tried to tell you over and

over that I didn't care. I just wanted you, us. But it's too late. My bags are packed. I've got a studio apartment near to college."

"Don't do this, Jess. Please."

"I've already done it. We're over."

I realised I'd stirred the coffee about ten times while lost in my thoughts. I'd not seen my husband in almost eight years, but he hadn't really changed. There was a worn look to his once youthful skin, but that was the only difference. He still wore his dark blonde hair short and the way his shirt and trousers hugged his body showed me he still probably trained at the gym.

Picking up the mugs, I walked back out to find him sitting on the sofa.

"So how come a Sergeant is handling something as simple as a broken window?" I asked.

"Withernsea and the surrounding areas have a severe shortage of policemen. It's all hands on deck here. No airs and graces or quoting rank."

"When did you start here?"

"Last week."

"I thought your father had finally given up. It's been eight years."

"In my father's life, eight years is no time at all, is it? When you're immortal, it must be the blink of an eye."

I sighed, taking a seat at the side of him. "I guess not."

"It's good to see you, Jess. You look really well. Looks like psychology was the right choice for you."

I nod. "It was. I love my work and I'm looking forward to this new venture."

"Me too. I guess we just have to get used to the fact we might bump into each other. Withernsea's not the largest of places."

"Yes, well, if you could tell your father to butt out." I told my ex.

"Oh, I intend to have a few words with the old man. Don't you worry. I can't believe we're both here by accident."

A yawn took over my mouth despite the coffee. "Well, he has Fate herself on speed dial. She's been very busy with my friend, but maybe she's decided to pick on me now."

"So being in my company is you being bullied?"

I sighed. "You know what I mean. It's a shock isn't it? It's a shock to me seeing you again. Almost as much as a shock as having my window broken."

Lachlan stood. "Well, I'm sure that was just

someone who's had a few too many, but obviously if you see or hear anyone else hanging around the place, just call us." He handed me a card. "That's my mobile number in case you need it."

I took it but didn't say anything further.

The buzzer sounded indicating the repair man was here. "I'll stay until the window is done."

I shook my head. "There's no need. I'm perfectly capable of looking after myself."

All the fight left him. His shoulders slumped and he turned to me. "Yes, that's something you've made perfectly clear." He didn't say goodnight. He just walked out, the door banging behind him. I heard him acknowledge the man at the bottom of the stairs. Then I put a smile on my face as I welcomed the man in.

Once the board was up and I was back left alone in my apartment, I sat down on my sofa and cried. For what I wasn't sure, but I fell asleep once I'd exhausted myself.

CHAPTER 8

Jessica

I woke to the sound of my alarm going off in the bedroom. Of course, I was still on the sofa, my face crumpled into the arm. As I sat up, I rubbed at my neck. I'd fallen asleep in the worst position, which meant moving my neck caused pain, and my eyes felt like I'd been punched in them. Dragging myself into the bedroom, I switched off the alarm and then I padded back into the kitchen to make a fresh pot of coffee. My eyes flicked to the coffee table where two mugs sat and I recalled Lachlan being on the sofa, then the look on his face before he left.

I wondered if he'd moved on at all. I guessed not if his father had engineered his move to Withernsea, and I knew I certainly hadn't. No matter how much

I'd tried to 'get back on the horse' and date, there was no one who'd kept my interest, who I'd loved as much as I'd loved my husband. It was just a shame he'd loved his job more.

After my coffee and a slice of toast and butter, I enjoyed a shower. Finally feeling more awake, I dressed in a white shirt and a pair of black slacks, applied light make-up and then I made my way through to Cupid Inc. Mabel was vacuuming the carpet when I arrived.

"What happened to your window?" She asked me.

"They think someone messing around, probably drunk. Early hours of this morning it happened." I shrugged my shoulders.

"Scummy bastards. Should be in bed at that time, not drinking. No respect for the place."

"Am I the first here?" I asked, looking at the clock on the wall. It was five past eight.

"You are, lovely. Go on through to your office and I'll make you a nice hot drink. What do you like?"

"A latte please. Jax's blend."

"Right, you go and get comfy ready for your first day and I'll bring you that drink shortly. It's strange not knowing what to expect isn't it? Whether we'll be busy or dead quiet." She paused. "Well, we'll not be dead quiet because Max works here, but you know what I mean."

"Morrrnnniiinggg beaaauuuttifffullll laaddi-ieeeees." Max sang as he walked through the door. He was wearing black jeans that looked sprayed on, and a silver shirt, plus a cowboy hat.

"Would you like a drink, Max, sweetie?" Mabel asked him.

"No thank you, darling. I already had three because I couldn't sleep after the whole window breaking debacle. Do you know who came to investigate? Jess' ex-husband."

Mabel swung around to look at me. "Really? Your ex?"

I rolled my eyes. "It appears he has a job here in Withernsea. It's my ex-father-in-law interfering."

"Cupid himself." Max filled Mabel in.

"Wow, I've certainly started work somewhere a lot more interesting than my last job at the Aldi. Hey, can I play some Christmas music in the reception if I keep it low?"

"Absolutely, and when Samara gets here, if she says otherwise, she's outvoted, okay, darling?" Max looked around. The front of Cupid Inc housed the reception desk at one side and then at the other there were another two desks. Samara and Max would take it in turns to work from behind reception while the other one took a desk. The other desk was for Rebecca's use. In front of the reception desk was a red comfy seating area and then a door at the back led through to a kitchen with a dining table; the bathroom; and my office with its own washroom facilities, there for any teary clients.

"Right, it's my turn to be on reception. I'm ready for my close-up." Max walked around and sat behind the desk. He picked up the silent phone making his own ringing sound. "Cupid Inc Dating Services. How may I help you?" He practiced. "You want me to help you get a date? You say you're undateable." He paused as Rebecca walked through the door. "Well as long as your name isn't Rebecca Wilkins you've called the right place."

I raised a brow.

"Impossible." He pointed to her. "Wouldn't wish that on my worst enemy."

"Morning everyone but my brother." Rebecca said, walking over to one of the desks, and dropping her bag off on the seat. "Well, what a surprise, Samara is the last to arrive. She's probably still in bed."

Mabel shook her head. "No, she's got a doctor's appointment. She'll be in around ten."

She looked at me. "Sorry, I was supposed to tell you when you arrived, but I got distracted by my excitement of our first day."

Rebecca put her hands on her hips. "Seriously, she's booked a GP appointment on our very first day? I don't know why they let her get away with all her crap."

"It's the first day, she's not done anything." I stuck up for my friend.

"Exactly. The lazy Cupid has not done, and probably won't, do anything; except try to make me look stupid. I know full well she's going to trawl through my past matches until she can dredge up some way of making me look bad."

"I think maybe we should try for at least one full working day before we start casting aspersions on colleagues." I said, trying to keep my temper.

"Now do you see what I was saying about trying to matchmake her up with anyone?" Max said. "Worse than being put on the rack. We should hire her out as a torture device."

"I can hear you." Rebecca said.

"You're meant to." Max shot back.

I rubbed at my forehead. "I'll be in my office if

anyone needs me."

"I'll be cleaning the kitchen." Mabel added.

We walked through the back door.

"Do you think they'll both still be alive when we surface?" I asked Mabel.

"They're siblings, they'll be absolutely fine."

"You sound like you have lots of experience in that department."

"I have five children and twelve grandchildren."

"Jesus. That must make for an expensive Christmas."

"It does, but it also makes for fantastic family get-togethers, so it's worth it. Do you have a big family?"

I shook my head. "Not really. My parents were only children. My grandma on my mother's side is still alive, but that's about it for family."

"Well there's time yet for your own family." She squeezed my arm.

"I don't know. The clock's ticking and I'm extremely single. Maybe I'll just become a cat lady and live with about twenty felines."

Later I'd experience Maisie again and change my mind vehemently.

I took a seat behind my new desk. My office smelled

divine with that new carpet smell. I powered up my laptop and checked my emails. There were a few queries from my old job so while I drank a nice hot drink, I dealt with those. I realised that I'd better bring a book or magazine for the first few days as while Max and Samara started on their new case-loads, I was unlikely to have a lot to do. Sitting back and sighing, I wondered if I had made a huge mistake in coming here. I'd wanted a fresh start and instead my fetid decomposed past had reared its head. It was time for my ex-father-in-law to be held to account. I called him direct.

"Jessica, darling. 8:20am. I've been expecting your call this morning. I've already heard from my son. Fancy you both being in Withernsea."

"Yes, fancy that. What a coincidence. I'm ringing to tell you I quit. Thanks for everything, but I want to leave. Are there any more openings within the Cupid enterprises before I start contacting agencies?"

"Oh, Jessica. Did you not think I'd anticipate that? You signed a contract stating you'd stay at least three months. Also, there's no time to replace you, so if you leave, Samara and Max will no doubt fail their probation periods. All because they lacked support."

I ground my fingernails into my left palm.

"Sounds like you have it all worked out, but the thing is, you can't make me and Lachlan fall back in love. It went wrong for a reason. We're not suited. You got it wrong."

"No, I didn't. I'm Cupid. I don't get matches wrong. I just happened to match two extremely stubborn people whose heads need banging together. Now if that's all, you're being paid to work aren't you, so you'd best get back to it."

"Uuurrrggghhh." I was so frustrated.

"Always a pleasure to hear your voice, lovely. Keep in touch. Speak soon." He ended the call.

I threw the phone across the room just as Max opened my door. He caught it and did a twirl.

"Hey, girlfriend. Want to talk about it?" He held up a hand as I started to speak. "But first, can we just talk about how amazing that catch was. I should be a cricketer, although I tried once and got thrown out for rubbing the ball on another cricketer's crotch instead of my own."

"Have you heard of knocking on a door?" I shouted.

"Ooooh. Is it that time of the month?" Max pulled a face and then pulled up a chair in front of me. "Tell Uncle Max all about it."

"There's nothing to tell. I'm just having a very

frustrating morning already."

Max raised a brow. "And it has nothing to do with a certain blonde-haired sex god who reappeared in your life in the early hours of the morning?"

"None at all." I jutted out my jaw.

"So it's work then?" He crossed a leg over the other and folded his arms across his chest. Then he smirked.

"Well, no. Oh, I don't want to talk about it. Can you get some clients so we can focus on their mental health and wellbeing?"

"I'm on it and that's why I've come in. Sorry about not knocking. I was excited. Maisie is coming in for an interview at 2pm. Can you sit in with me because I'm doing her preliminary interview for matches, going over her application she gave the Dating Agency and reviewing her dates so far. I need you there to see if there's anything blocking her from dating and also because she scares me."

I laughed. "I'll be there."

It wasn't like I had anything else to do and maybe I could genuinely help Maisie find a date. I needed to throw myself into this whole Cupid Inc thing so that my friends could pass their probation periods and I could help others find love, even if it wasn't in my own future.

CHAPTER 9

Samara

My doctor had confirmed that I was pregnant. I'd been given a midwife appointment and would be booked in to have my early dating scan in a couple of weeks. I was buzzing, but Johnny and I still agreed that we wouldn't tell anyone else our news until I passed the twelve-week mark.

I walked into the Cupid Inc office feeling so happy. I had a gorgeous husband, a baby on the way, and a new job. Unfortunately, the first thing I met was the cloud of doom sitting at the desk next to mine. Talk about rain on my parade.

"Good afternoon." Rebecca said. I would have said she spoke snarkily but that was her usual tone.

"It's one minute past ten."

"We all started at eight."

"I've had a doctor's appointment." I placed my bag down and hung up my coat.

"Oh yeah? Playing doctors and nurses with your husband more like."

I looked around. "Where's Max? Isn't he supposed to be on reception?"

"He's just popped in to see Jessica about an appointment he's booked for this afternoon. Anyway, my files are waiting on your desk. Don't expect to find anything you can ruin me with. Sorry, but I'm going to have to disappoint you as I'm good at what I do."

I sat down. "Oh I know. You're amazing at your job. I don't expect to turn up anything at all, and then I can just move on to looking after my own past matches."

Rebecca eyed me suspiciously. "You can't fool me. I know you're going to try to embarrass me or get me to fail in front of Cupid."

"Rebecca. You have me all wrong. I know we've never particularly got along but I accept now that you are an amazing Point and Shoot Cupid. I'll have a tiny look over your files, where I'm sure I'll find nothing and then I'll be sure to tell Cupid that you're amazing. Like he said, we should make sure to get along. It's best for the future of Cupid Inc."

She peered at me, her eyes looking me over. "Have you got a twin? It's not you, is it, Samara? Or a doppelganger. Or maybe you've been possessed."

"Morrnnniinnggg, Samaaarrrraaa." Max glided out of the back and took his place behind the reception desk. "Huge gossip already. Jess had her window broken last night and the cop who came to investigate was her ex-husband."

My eyes widened. "Really? What's he like?"

"Ooh, you're going to get to see first-hand." Max pulled a compact from behind the reception desk and fluffed up his hair. "He just parked in the car park out front. He's on his way in."

All three of us watched the policeman approach our offices. He pushed open the door. Mabel came bounding out of the back and ground to a halt.

"Oh."

In fact, as I looked around all four of us were standing there with our mouths hanging open while Jess' ex stood cocking a hip. "Good morning, Lachlan. How can I help you today? Is it police business or matters of the heart?" Max smiled.

"What would you like to drink, dearie? You upholders of the law need to keep your strength up.

I'll get you a biscuit too." Mabel seemed all of a dither.

Rebecca moved out from her desk and stalked over to Lachlan. I think she was attempting to do a sexy wiggle, but she looked like she was badly in need of a wee. "Hi, I'm Rebecca." She held out a hand.

Lachlan exhaled, but took it. "Sergeant Lachlan Hart. Is Jessica Hart here?"

"We have a Jessica Fazakerley..."

He huffed. His jaw set and jutting out. A pulse ticked in his cheek.

"I need to see Miss Fazakerley," He spat her surname out, "regarding an incident in the early hours of this morning."

"I'll just go and get her." I told him. "Take a seat and Mabel will be getting you that drink."

Walking through to the back I knocked softly on Jessica's door.

"Come in." She said. There was an underlying tension to her tone.

I walked through, seeing that tension holding her body hostage. Heading straight up to her, I placed my arms around her shoulders, giving her a squeeze. "You okay? I hear there's been some shit happening."

She sighed.

I walked back around the front of her desk and took a seat. "Spill."

"Never mind me. How did you get on this morning? And how are you feeling?"

"I was nauseous first thing, but it's passed off at the moment. Doctor confirmed the pregnancy. I shall be a mummy in July."

"Oh, Samara. That's wonderful. Congratulations."

"Thank you. We're going to keep it quiet for a few more weeks."

"My lips are sealed."

"Anyway, back to you. I want full details of your reunion with Sergeant Hart."

Her back stiffened. "How do you know my ex's surname?"

"Because, sweetie, he's currently sitting in reception waiting to see you."

Jessica ran her fingers through her hair. "For God's sake. What does he want now?"

"Well, by the way he spat out your maiden name, I'd say you."

Jessica froze in her chair for a moment before her eyes met mine.

"Well, that ship sailed a long, long time ago."

"Hmm, don't think he got the memo. So anyway, what happened last night? I saw the window was boarded up. I just thought Max had visited and had been singing again."

That made a smile come to my friend's lips. "Just some stupid youths, I think. Probably thought the building was still empty. Threw a brick. No big deal except it made me jump. And then of course it brought my ex in. I've spoken to Cupid this morning. He's done it deliberately. Says we need our heads banging together and that we are destined. He can't accept that once he got it wrong. Maybe because it was his son's match he messed up? We aren't meant to be."

A knock came at the door and Max's voice sounded through. "Sergeant Hart is in reception waiting."

I stood up. "Me and you are going out to Jetty's for lunch and you're going to tell me everything. Then, if it's definitely all over I'll help you in getting that message through to Cupid. Now, are you okay seeing your ex or shall I tell him to send someone else?"

"No, send him through. I'm going to have to get used to seeing him around if we live in the same area. I might as well start now."

"You sure?" I checked one last time.

"No; but send him in anyway." She sighed.

I almost fell over Max outside the door. "Did you find out any juicy scandal?"

"No." His face fell. "But I will." I winked.

"Goody."

We walked back into the reception area. I found Rebecca sitting on the edge of her desk. Her skirt had ridden higher up her thigh.

"Oh, Lachlan, you are amusing." She said, flicking her hair.

"Well, if you find local crime rates entertaining." He said, his brow creasing.

"It's your voice, it just comes out so... captivating."

"If you'd like to come through, Sergeant." I beckoned him towards the back rooms.

"Lachlan. You can call me Lachlan." He stood up and I realised he was almost a foot taller than I was. I felt safe and protected just by him standing tall.

We walked through to the corridor and I turned to him. "Before you go in, Jessica is my friend. I know you have a past. Please tread carefully with her. She's not as strong as she makes out to be."

Lachlan huffed. "I used to think I knew her inside out. Every molecule of her. But I guess I was wrong. I'm here on business. That's all." We reached Jessica's office and I left him to knock on her door.

Returning to my desk I wondered how to respond to Rebecca's flirting with Jess' ex. I didn't want to argue with her, I wanted her out of Withernsea. I decided to start going through the files. The quicker I praised her to Cupid, and she got promoted out of here the better. Plus, if Jess still did have any feelings for Lachlan, it wouldn't hurt for a little of the green-eyed monster to surface. And Rebecca did have green eyes...

Later, I called through to Cupid Inc Headquarters and asked to speak to the man himself while Rebecca was out doing her pointing and shooting. Surprisingly he was available to speak to there and then.

"Well good morning, Samara. How goes the first few hours of my new venture?"

"I can't complain. I've begun to look at Rebecca's books." I lied. I'd so far only chatted with my colleagues. "I actually don't think I'm going to find much, if anything, there. She actually seems really good at her job. Top notch in fact. Just this morning she's shot her arrow at two couples. I think she's wasted here in Withernsea."

"Really? You deduced that already? Well, all your probation periods are at the very least a month long, so we'll just have to see if you carry on thinking she's amazing. I'm sure your friendship will thrive if you tell her so."

Fuck. He wasn't falling for it.

"Yes, I'll make sure to do so." *After Hell freezes over*.

"Will that be all, Samara?"

I sighed. "Yes. I just called to sing my colleague's praises."

"Well, maybe we could have an employee of the week. I'll let you organise it, shall I? You could nominate Rebecca this week. I could send a prize, like a trophy to put on the desk all week."

"Oh, I think someone's coming in, I'll have to go." I said quickly.

A deep chuckle came down the line.

"I'm only messing you with you, sweetpea. Now play nice with Rebecca. I'm glad you called anyway. I was going to give you a couple of days to settle in, but seeing as you're on the line…"

"Yes?"

"You have your first aftercare project. He'll have just come in."

"We haven't had any customers come in yet, unless of course someone has just walked in since I've been in the office. I'd better go check."

"Oh no. Fate told me my son is already there and should currently be talking to his ex-wife, my ex-daughter-in-law."

"What do you mean my first aftercare project?"

"Oh didn't I mention it before? You see I've only ever failed with a match once, in that something went wrong and for some reason that I've never been able to get to the bottom of, two people who are absolutely perfect for each other broke up. Now I'm Cupid. I don't make errors, so your first proper job other than seeing what amazing work Rebecca has done is to re-unite Jessica and Lachlan."

"Are you freaking kidding me?" I yelled. "That's not fair."

"Well, if you're worthy of your role-and you told

me aftercare was what you wanted to do-you'll do your best to re-unite them or you'll come back to tell me, Cupid, that I made a mistake. Anyway, you need to do this to pass your probation. Call it your entrance exam. Oh, I think someone's coming in, I'll have to go." He parroted back at me and ended the call.

"Gaaaaaaahhhh." I screamed.

Max ran towards me from the reception desk and held out his hands. He was standing determined like a goalkeeper in a World Cup final.

"What are you doing?"

"I'm getting ready to save the phone. I thought you were going to throw it like Jess did hers earlier."

I placed the phone that I almost had thrown down.

I now had a waiting game until Lachlan left Jess' office and I took her to lunch to get the low-down on their relationship. Cupid had put me in a very awkward position, and I hoped that nothing I did would spoil the friendship Jess and I had established. Until then I needed to go through the files that Rebecca had left. While I quickly looked through them it crossed my mind that if I'd had anything to hide, I would have made sure to not pass it on, but to try and act stupid if found out. I therefore printed off a list of matches so I could cross them off my list as I checked each file.

Perfect Princess Rebecca was probably squeakly clean, but I was going to look for the dirt anyway. Just in case my plan to get rid of her didn't wash.

CHAPTER 10

Jessica

I didn't know how to school my expression for seeing my ex-husband again, so I left the naturally weary look on my face as I invited him in and asked him to take a seat.

"I thought you'd have finished your shift by now." I queried.

"I'm working a double with us being short-staffed."

"Ah."

"What do you mean 'ah'?" He bristled. "Every single thing you say sounds loaded, like it means something else. Takes me right back."

"I meant of course you're working a double shift. You probably never actually stop. That's what takes *me* right back."

"I don't want to fight with you, Jess." He rubbed the scruff that was starting to build up on his chin because he'd not been home to shave. I preferred him with it, but I'd never get to tell him that. It wasn't my place. The thought that one day it might be some other woman's place made my insides twist.

"So are you okay after the broken window? There have been no more disturbances?"

"No, everything's been fine. I'm fine."

"There was nothing on the scene to give any indication as to who could have done it."

"Let's just put it down to kids unless anything else happens then, yes? And let's get back to normal."

There was a pause.

"What is our normal now then?"

I sighed. "I don't know. Maybe we agree to be civil to one another? I'm here for at least three months, so we're going to bump into one another. Maybe we just take it one day at a time, huh?"

"Yeah, one day at a time."

He stood up from his seat.

"Well, I'll keep the file open for a week or so and then if there's nothing else, I'll close the case." He went into his pocket and took out his business card. "Just in case you didn't keep the last one, or maybe you can keep one here and one at home. Call me if you need assistance."

"Wouldn't I call 999?"

"If it's an emergency yes. Then after you can call me. Whatever our past, I'd always be there for you if you needed me. If you were in any danger," he added quickly.

I was in danger okay, but the only person causing it was the man who still held my heart in his hands even if he didn't know it.

He left and despite the fact the clock said it was twelve thirty, I felt like I'd been at work for two years. Samara came to the door that Lachlan had left ajar and she leant on the doorframe. "Get your coat, we're going to Jetty's for lunch."

I went to open my mouth to say I didn't feel like it, but Samara gave me some serious side-eye.

"Get. Your. Coat."

"Okay, okay." I said standing up. "Keep your knickers on."

"I'm not wearing any, babes." She answered winking.

"And now I need an exorcist to get that visual

right out of my mind. You've put me off my lunch." I moaned.

"I'm joking with you. I have my enormous Bridget Jones style pants on. I went to the doctors remember? I have to at least pretend to be respectable."

Samara

We left a pouting Max on reception who whined loudly about having to stay to look after the office while we went out without him and we walked up the road to the ice-cream parlour. Of course, they still sold ice-cream given that was their main income, but with it being winter, they diversified with a line of toasties and warm waffles.

A tall, thin male came over to us. I'd have described him as brooding. Not so much with dark good looks but rather with the surly look on his face.

"Welcome to Jetty's. What can I get you?" He said in a flat tone, sounding more like a robot than a waiter.

Jess and I exchanged glances. "If I could have a water please, and Jess?"

"Mocha for me with one sugar please."

"Any food?"

"Cheese and tomato toastie."

"Make that two."

"Is that everything?" The robotic waiter asked before leaving to take our orders through to the back.

"Laugh a minute that one, isn't he?" I nodded in his direction. "What with him here and Sir Loins being all miserable at Jax's."

"Sir Loins?"

"Oh I forget you've not been there yet. He's the barista there. Just broken up with his girlfriend and he's miserable. I bet that's what's happened to this guy too."

"Maybe."

"I'm going to try to find out. Maybe he's a potential aftercare client?"

"Well, be careful. I don't want him spitting in my dinner."

The waiter brought our drinks over. Between him going to get my water and coming back I now really wanted a lemonade, at a like my-life-depended-on-it level.

"Ooh, can I have a lemonade please? With lots of ice."

"You want another drink?" Grumpy pointed to my water.

"Yes, and lots of ice. Don't forget the ice." He sighed and stomped off.

Jessica smiled. "Are you having cravings?"

I grinned. "I think I am." I had a quick gulp of water. "So, what did Lachlan have to say?"

She sighed. "Do we have to do this? Are you going to make me talk about him?"

"Abso-fucking-lutely. You have met me, haven't you? I want to know everything. What happened today, where you met. Everything."

The waiter came back with my lemonade.

"Do you have any lemons to go with it?"

He pointed to the drink. "There's a slice of lemon in it."

"No, it's not enough. Do you have like, erm, eight slices of lemon. Yes, eight. That should be okay." I picked out the slice of lemon and ate all the inside and then I started crunching on an ice cube.

"Okay, which species are you then if you don't mind me asking because I've seen some strange shit in here, but people eating lemon and crunching ice cubes without pulling a face. That's a new one."

I beckoned him closer with my finger. "It's a secret at the moment but I'm a pregnant species." I confessed. I was surprised when a smile came to his face.

"Ah, I should have guessed. My sister was weird then too. Eight slices of lemon coming up." He said and he disappeared back behind the counter.

"Well, from looking like he was sucking them to willingly slicing them up for you." Jessica pointed out.

"You get a lot of special treatment being pregnant. I'm going to make the most of it." I laughed.

I thought Jess would laugh back but instead she said. "Just go careful, it's still very early days."

I took a punt. "You sound like you're speaking from experience." As I watched her face, Jess' eyes welled up and she swallowed.

"It was a long time ago now and I wasn't pregnant long enough for it to count, if at all."

I reached out and held my hand over hers. "Every pregnancy counts, Jess. No matter how long for. Tell me about it, please."

She took a deep breath and spoke in a low, soft voice. "If I do, you mustn't say a word because no one knows."

"No one? Not even the father knew?"

Jess shook her head. "No. Because I did a test

one day and the next I bled, so maybe it was a false positive anyway. I'll never know."

"Was it Lachlan's?"

Her eyes fixed on mine. "Yes. But he was at work as usual when it all happened. I tried to tell him, but he was too busy."

"That's when you left him, isn't it?"

She nodded, staring into space before returning her gaze to me. "He had no idea what was going on right around him. He could only think about his job and promotion. He was so busy looking to the future he let the present go."

"Oh, Jess. I am so very sorry you had to go through all that alone. I'm sorry for chatting on about being pregnant. It must be hard."

"Oh God, no. Don't you dare pussyfoot around me and apologise for your happiness. I'm thrilled for you. My situation wasn't meant to be. I made my peace with it all eight years ago. I believe that whether I was pregnant or not, the situation was sent to me to show me that I needed to move on with my life. I moved and passed my exams and never looked back."

"Really?"

She sighed. "Okay, I looked back and wondered where it all went wrong."

"And?"

"I don't know. I'm not sure when we changed course to a path of destruction. We were good and then we weren't."

"Do you still love him?"

She shrugged. "What does it matter? We don't work together."

"You did once."

The waiter came over with eight slices of lemon, an extra bowl of ice cubes, and another lemonade. "On the house," he said smiling. "Got to look after the little one."

I turned green as I got a whiff of the lemon. "Erm, actually..."

"I'm here, bitches." Max came through the door and scraped a chair back at the side of us, plonking himself down. "Finally, my sister returned so I could get out to join you. Girls, what's with all the lemon, ARE WE HAVING TEQUILA?"

"No, Max. Just lemonade."

"Oh, you disappoint me. I thought we could get pissed up and then I might have the nerve to deal with my client."

"What is your problem with Maisie? She's really nice."

He tilted his head at me. "If she's so nice, why can't she find a date?"

"She just has some unusual tendencies."

"Like being a bitch." Max quipped. He clicked his fingers in the direction of the waiter who went back to his previous surly expression and took his time, serving another three tables before finally coming over. "Can I help you?" He said tersely.

"Oh yeah, can I have a coke float please and your phone number?"

I elbowed him in the side violently. "Max, enough." I turned to the waiter. "I am so sorry for my friend's high level of inappropriateness. He was joking. We're leaving."

Max's hands went to his hips. "I haven't had my coke float."

"It's almost time for your appointment with Maisie, so let's go."

He climbed up on a chair in the corner of the parlour. "I'm not going, you can't make me."

"I'll just send Maisie in here then, shall I? You can see her without Jess."

He slowly got down. "You are not nice, Samara Leighton." He huffed. "Now do you think that guy got a good look at my butt from my position on the chair? It's a great angle, right?"

As we made our way back to the office, Max kept us all entertained, but I could see Jess' smiles did not reach her eyes. I decided then that I would definitely do my best to re-unite her and Lachlan; not because Cupid commanded it, but because she was my friend and deserved her own happiness.

CHAPTER 11

Jessica

Max had actually done me a favour coming in when he had. The conversation had been heavy, and I'd not planned on sharing my secrets, but Samara just had that friendly way about her that made you open up. I knew she wouldn't say anything to anyone else. I was glad we had Maisie coming in for an appointment that afternoon. It would take my mind off Lachlan for an hour or so, because since I'd seen him, I'd found it hard to think about much else. The man came to replace the glass in my window and Samara offered to stay in my apartment while the job was done seeing as we had Maisie due at any moment. When it got to ten past two, I went out to the reception to make sure Max wasn't being held prisoner by his next appointment.

But there was no one there except Max who was singing *Away in a Manger*.

"No sign of your appointment."

"Nope. Looks like she bailed." He spun on his office chair.

"There's no need to look so pleased. She's part of your probation period, remember?"

"Hmm, I feel like I'm being set up to fail. I will have to find a date for someone else." He narrowed his eyes in my direction. "Would you consider yourself undateable, Jess?"

"No." I caught sight of Maisie walking very slowly up the street towards us. "Anyway, she's here."

We watched as she sauntered. She was dressed in tight black leggings, long black boots up to her thighs, and a black t-shirt with rips across the chest that revealed the top of her breasts. She was overtly sexual and the kind of woman that you wanted to hate because they were so bloody attractive. She pushed open the door of the building and leaned on the reception counter. "I have an appointment with you." She said to Max.

"You're late." Max told her.

She shrugged her shoulders. "Ever seen a cat wear a watch? Me neither."

"Come through to my office, Maisie. It's more private." We'd just have to leave the reception locked until Samara came back down. I couldn't see us being inundated with disappointed visitors anyway if the morning had been anything to go by.

In my office, Maisie went straight over to the couch and curled up with her feet under her.

I pulled a chair up near her and gestured to Max to do the same. He sat in front of her with his folder, and a pen that had a sparkly fake diamond on the end and fake pink feathers.

"So, Mais. If I could go through your form."

"Okay, Cedric."

"Sorry, Mais. What?"

"I said, okay, *Cedric.*"

"My name's not Cedric."

"My name isn't Mais."

"And this is why you're undateable." Max blurted out. "I've heard the others call you Mais. You're just being sly and awkward."

She stretched out on the couch and yawned.

I leant over to Max. "Pet her."

"You fucking what?" He whisper-shouted.

"She's a cat. Want to get around her? Pet her. Treat her like a cat, not a person. What have you got to lose?"

"My beautiful face if she claws me to death?"

He huffed loudly. "What-ev-er." Standing up he walked over to Maisie who eyed him suspiciously. He held out a hand towards her. "Your hair is beautiful, Maisie. Can I stroke it?"

"You may."

He stroked down her hair and made gagging motions to me from behind her. "Lovely cat. Now would you like some milk before we start?"

"Do you have any fish?" Maisie asked.

"I'm afraid not because it's a dating agency not a fish and chip shop." He caught my glare and jumped up. "I'll just get your milk."

When he left I turned to Maisie. "Stop tormenting him; you've had your fun now."

She pouted. "But it's so much fun."

"Yeah, well do you want a date or not? It's all very well being aloof, demanding, and cat like, but it's not going to get you anyone who wants to stay around."

"Yeah, well that's the story of my life. No one ever does. Not my parents who didn't want to know when I got bitten, even though they'd taken the stray werecat in in the first place. Then I finally found Frankie, but he wasn't interested once he settled down with Lucy; and the next-door-neighbours, well as soon as they got pregnant, it was bye bye. So what is the point? I get settled somewhere and then thrown out with last night's newspapers."

Well we certainly appeared to be getting straight to the root cause of Maisie's difficulties. She didn't trust that anyone would stick around. "Look, give Max a chance. He's going to do his best to find you your perfect match and I will work with you about how to accept that you can't ever know if someone will stay around. You have to be happy in yourself and enjoy what joy you can take from each day."

"You're single, aren't you? It sucks, end of."

"Yeah, you're totally right," I agreed. "But you can still either play the victim or get on with life. I choose to get on with life."

"Okay." Maisie sat up as Max walked back in. She took the cup of milk from him and lapped it up with her tongue. I watched Max shudder.

"Okay, Max. What do you want to know?" She said.

When he'd gathered up all his information, he told Maisie he would be in touch very soon with details of her first date. Max would do a pre-date appointment, discussing potential conversational topics. Then the date would take place and if there were any problems, the date would be curtailed, and

Maisie would come back to the office to speak with us.

"I really don't know why I'm single." Maisie said. "I like men and women, so I have twice as many people to choose from." She started coughing. Great big wracking coughs and eventually she hurled up a hairball. Max started to gag. "Okay so maybe that's why." She said, grabbing a tissue off my desk and picking it up. "It's not exactly sexy, is it?"

"We'll get there, Maisie. I promise." I told her, but neither of us looked particularly convinced in light of the hairball incident.

"So who are you going to set her up with first?" I asked Max.

"Bartholomew Simpson, the barista at Jax's. He's newly single and he's hot. If nothing else she can let him roger her senseless. Plus, she can get staff discount on her daily saucer of milk. It's a winner."

Max soon lived to regret his over-confidence.

Two days later Maisie came into the office. Her face had three big scratches down her right cheek and her top lip was bust up.

"Maisie. What the hell happened?" I asked. I'd only come out to reception to grab a coffee.

"Is Max in?" She hissed. "Only I'd like to update him about what happens when you set a werecat up with a barista, and his jealous ex doesn't like it and attacks you."

"He's at a meeting with Shelley." I looked around wondering where Samara was and then I heard the sounds of retching in the background. I turned the reception's Christmas music up. "Oh dear. I guess she must have had some false nails on her?"

"She's a werewolf. One of the toughest there is. She brought down a whole pack on her own. I didn't even like her stupid boyfriend because that's what he is. Stupid. I asked him if he wanted to to hang out at The Marine and he said yes and untucked his shirt. Then Alyssa, that's his ex, turned up. I went outside and asked what business of hers it was if he was single and got this for my troubles. Anyway, they're back together so at least one union came out of it."

It brought out a whole new meaning to swipe right, that was for sure.

"Come through to my office and take a seat, Maisie. Let's chat some more while you are here."

She hesitated and then walked over to the couch and curled up on it again. "Don't suppose you want a resident cat? Only this couch is amazing."

"Maisie. Why do you not get your own place? With a nice comfy couch?"

She sighed. "Because I like to be looked after. Petted. Spoiled. If I live on my own, then there's no one to do those things for me. I hate it at the moment, now Frankie and Lucy are away travelling, and the neighbours don't want me around anymore. The restaurants chase me off nine times out of ten. I've started hanging around at the grooming salon because that new woman is kind, but I have to be careful because they largely cater for dogs."

Like all of us, Maisie was just looking for love, care, and companionship. Her brittle edge and cat-like qualities of aloofness no doubt put people off, but underneath she really was a pussy cat.

"When Max comes in, I'll help him go through the dating agency books and see if we can't find something different to what you've been originally matched with. It can happen a lot with mixed species. Your dating agency results are skewed by the different qualities you have. Plus, sometimes people complete their application forms without being brutally honest."

"I might need to do mine again." She admitted. "At least to state a clear dislike of other female's claws."

. . .

When Maisie had left, I went to check on Samara who now looked grey but was eating a doughnut.

"Are you okay?"

"Sure. You?"

"I'm thinking that maybe I need to go on a date, soon."

Samara perked up. "Seriously? You feel ready to embrace love again?"

"I've done nothing but feel sorry for myself since I got here, and well, also for the last eight years since things with me and Lachlan went wrong. Then I was talking to Maisie this morning and even having been almost taken out by a werewolf hasn't deterred her from wanting to find love and companionship. I don't think I should be sitting every night in my apartment above my workplace, listening to Max's warbling coming from across the hall. I need to be enjoying myself. If not dating then doing something to get to know my new surroundings better."

"Have you visited the lighthouse yet?" Withernsea had a lighthouse museum as its main tourist attraction.

I shook my head.

"Well, it's only £3 to get in so why not start

there? Let me look at the opening times for you." Samara began typing furiously into the keypad. She seemed very determined I should see it; it must be good. "It closes at 5pm on a weekday so you'd have to go Saturday or Sunday? Which would be better?"

"I think I'll go Saturday. What time?"

"It's 1pm until 5pm. I could meet you there if you like?"

"Are you sure? Won't you have couply things to do?"

She shook her head. "No, Johnny will be fine on his own for a bit. I'll spend some time with you. Like you said you're settling in and I should help you do that. We could go to Jax's after."

I smiled. "That sounds great. Thank you so much. I feel better for making some plans for the weekend. I'm determined not to wallow in that flat and to live my life."

And next week I would get up the confidence to ask a guy out on a date. Waiter guy was handsome. Maybe I'd start there?

If all else failed there were two Cupids at my disposal and a dating agency nearby.

CHAPTER 12

Samara

*P*hew. Operation Cupid was in process. I'd sorted out one half of the equation. Now how to get the other half there. A couple of days ago I'd waited in Jessica's apartment while her bedroom window got replaced and it had given me the ideal opportunity to have a little nosy around. As soon as window guy left, I'd headed straight to the bottom of her wardrobe where sure enough I found a box with wedding photos and other bits in it.

The photos choked me up because both of them looked so damn happy. Completely and utterly in love. I could detect no single tingles from either of them in real life because they had already been matched and shot. They really did belong together. Life had just got in the way for both of them.

However, they had serious hurdles to overcome before they could move forward.

But if I could get over my husband having been turned into a Whippet for a time then I was sure I could sort these two out. As I'd looked through the photos there had been a lot of the two of them sight-seeing. In the photos they'd been younger and I assumed that they'd done this when they'd first got together, long before Lachlan started taking his work far too seriously and Jess had given up.

Somehow, I knew I needed to engineer them into this kind of situation, to remind them what they used to do. And I needed to act quickly now Jessica had announced she was ready to start dating again. The last thing I needed was for her to hurtle into a relationship that wasn't going to work.

Max returned to the office from meeting Shelley.

"How are things?" I asked him.

He sighed. "Not ideal. I need to meet with Jess for an hour because Maisie's date left her a bit sore and not in a good way."

I had no idea what he was talking about but seeing as that went for 3/4 of his conversations I just nodded and followed him down the corridor to Jess' office. He knocked and I followed him in.

"Why don't I look after all the phones while you

discuss things?" I said to them. "Work wise, I'm only still at the stage of looking through Rebecca's files, and so far, everything is in order."

"That would be great because I'm expecting a call from my mum. If you could answer and say 'Max Wilkin's assistant' so she can think I'm a success, and you can say I'm busy on a trip to Paris or something, so I don't have to speak to her either. Thanks, babes, that would just be epic."

I rolled my eyes.

"I'm okay. I'm not really expecting any calls." Jess told me.

Damn. I needed her phone. Luckily, Max being the diva he is inadvertently came to my rescue.

"Jess, darling. I need all your attention. I'm on probation and pussy is just not my specialty. We need to get Maisie her ideal date and fast."

I held my hand out for her phone, and sighing she passed it to me.

As soon as I was back out in reception, I typed a message to the phone number Lachlan had left on his business card.

Jessica: We need to talk. I'll be at With-

ernsea Lighthouse at 1pm on Saturday. Don't message me back, I won't reply. If you're interested in us moving forward, you'll be there.

I pressed send, deleted it from the sent folder and hoped to God he listened and didn't reply. Nothing came through for the next hour which made me think it could be okay.

I once more sat with the folders given to me by Rebecca and cross-referenced them against my print off. This time I found I had a match on my list that I did not have a file on. I felt excitement fizzing in my stomach. Well it was either that or too much antacid this morning. I clicked into the database for more information.

Holden Bisley
   Julie-Ann Lane

. . .

Matched and point and clicked August 2017 by Rebecca Wilkins.

Outcome: Not together. Anomaly. RW

An anomaly? Like as in she'd got it wrong and they weren't a match? It definitely warranted further investigation. Cupid wasn't moving Rebecca to London for her brilliance so I had no choice but to try to find dirt and use Cupid as a stain remover, preferably Vanish. I called the telephone number we had on the system for Julie-Ann.

"Hello, Nails by Julie-Ann."

Perfect. I could get a manicure at the same time as some information.

"Oh hello there. Could you tell me if having your nails done is safe when you are expecting a baby?"

"Yes, although you should always be cautious around fumes."

"Hmmm, could I maybe just book in with you for a straight French Polish then?"

"Of course. I'm a mobile technician so when would you like me to come around?"

Even more perfect. I wouldn't have to move. "When's the earliest you could come? I'm going out to an awards ceremony on Friday evening, so the sooner the better." I lied. "I'll pay you extra for your trouble..."

Thursday night Julie-Ann Lane was at my door. I'd asked Johnny to make himself scarce, so he'd gone down to The Marine to have a few pints with his friends. He'd not needed much encouragement. I didn't blame him. A night with me was usually a night accompanied by random moments of vomiting. I'd be glad when this stage passed that was for sure.

Julie-Ann was a friendly looking petite brunette with long glossy hair and a pout. She obviously enjoyed looking her best, care of fillers and fake tan.

"Samara?"

"Yes, come in. Would you like a drink?"

"Just a water please."

I directed her into the kitchen, and we sat at the kitchen table after I'd got us both some water. We made polite chit chat about my pregnancy and then I was able to ask about her love life after I told her where I worked.

"I'm single unfortunately. I can't get a past love out of my head. Stupid isn't it?"

Actually, it was perfect.

"Oh no. Was it a bad break up?" I asked.

"He moved to Denmark. Just like that." She looked wistful and started staring into space rather than polishing my nails. "I'd thought he was the one, you know? Then I got a card from Moonpig. Couldn't even write me a note or call me. Just said he'd had the offer of a lifetime and he couldn't turn it down."

My records gave no indication of Holden having moved to Denmark. His current address was in Hull.

"Anyway, I've dated since, but I've never felt the same way about any of them, so I've chosen to stay single. Unless my heart pounds the way it did every time I met Holden, I'm not interested. I often wonder what he's doing now. I bet he met a Danish woman and had beautiful babies."

"Well, if you wanted, I could check our database to see if I could find him? You'd have to fill out the proper forms, but maybe he's still single and I can get you guys back together?"

Her eyes lit up. "Seriously? Where are the forms? At least I'd get to know one way or another and that way if he is married and has children, I can finally lay that ghost to rest and move on with my life."

"I just so happen to have some forms in my bag."

I told her. "As soon as my nails are dry, we'll get things in motion."

An hour later I had gorgeous nails and a completed application form. Soon I would have my first Aftercare project complete, I had no doubt. But now I needed to investigate Holden Bisley. To find out why he'd ended things with Julie-Ann, if he was still single, and why Rebecca didn't want me to know about them.

"How did you get my number?" He spat down the line on Friday morning.

Uh oh. "I'm a private investigator so I have lots of contacts at my disposal not easily found by others." I lied. Max's eyes burned holes through me as he mouthed 'Tell me'. I nodded and carried on listening to a panic-stricken man.

"Oh God. Did she find me? I knew I'd not moved far enough away. She'd promised she'd leave me alone. I told her I moved to Denmark for Christ's sake. Then there was the restraining order. I mean she almost lost her job."

Oh dear. It appeared the reason the match hadn't gone so well was because one half was a stalker. She'd seemed so nice too.

"I'm sorry. I'll tell Julie-Ann I was unable to find you. Once again, please accept my apologies and—"

"Did you say Julie-Ann? Julie-Ann Lane?"

"Yes, why who did you think I meant?" But as I said the words, I knew his answer.

"Rebecca Wilkins."

I finished my phone call satisfied that I would definitely get my first Aftercare success, and if I wanted, I could potentially destroy Rebecca's career.

Max was like an excited puppy dancing at the side of me. "Tell me. Tell me what that phone call was about. I can smell gossip, it's like pheromones to me." He sniffed the air and went, "mmmmmm."

"You have to promise not to say a word, and it's going to be difficult because it involves your sister."

"Scout's honour." Max pulled Rebecca's seat up to my desk.

"Okay. So when I went through the paperwork there was a couple Rebecca hadn't included. Turns out your sister stalked one of them to the point he pretended to move away."

Max's forehead creased. "But the database would show her he didn't."

"Ah yes, but I believe her access to his details is restricted. Holden says that she almost lost her job."

"Holden? Is his surname Bisley?"

"Yes, why?"

"He was her first crush. Lived on the next street to us. He was two years above her at school."

"Well, what I can't work out is that despite the fact Holden and his match Julie-Ann were smitten and have never stopped thinking about each other, they've never got together. Both were told by your sister that the other had moved away, and somehow, they've never been able to find each other. Things just aren't adding up. Anyway, I've arranged for them to meet tomorrow evening at The Marine. Do you want to come and witness my first success?"

"Hell, yeah, baby girl, and also can we eat there? Been told the veggie sausage and mash is amazing and I love me some sausage." He accompanied this statement with a perverted style laugh.

"So you know how my side of things are progressing; how goes it with Maisie? We need to make sure she meets her own match."

"I could always strike one and set her on fucking fire."

"Max!"

"Well, she went out last night to meet a guy

called Steve and walked straight back out of the bar because he wore Hush Puppies and she won't have anything whatsoever to do with dogs."

"Oh God. Something will come to you, I'm sure. Or maybe you'll have to come to my team and undateables really are that—undateable."

"No. I refuse to believe it. I will find her something if it kills her."

"I don't think that's how that saying goes."

"Well it opens up more possibilities if she's a ghost."

"Yep, don't think the police will buy that excuse for murdering a client somehow."

"Ooh. Talking about cops. Has there been any progress with Jessica and the sexy sergeant?"

"Nope." I said while I considered confessing all.

"Samara Leighton. You have that look on your face that you get when you're being naughty. Spill, girlfriend. What have you done?"

Damn it. "Okay, so I've arranged to meet Jess tomorrow to show her the lighthouse."

"Erm, okay. I don't have to go do I?"

"No. I'm not going either."

"Okay, this is a very confusing conversation. It reminds me of my mother trying to explain to me why Rebecca could grow a moustache and I couldn't. Dark hair versus light. Makes such a difference."

"Max."

"Okay, okay. Carry on."

"I'm not going, but... I sent a message from Jess' phone asking Lachlan to meet her there to talk."

Max got his phone out of his pocket and did his fake ringing noise.

"Is that Withernsea Funeral Directors? I'd like to book an advance slot for Saturday, just after 1pm probably." He quipped.

"Samara, what were you thinking? She'll kill you."

"Well I have no choice do I because Cupid himself has decided that Jess and Lachlan are one of my cases."

He did a dramatic jaw drop and then placing his hand under his chin he closed his mouth.

"Suddenly, my quest to get Maisie a date seems so much easier." He smiled at me. "Good luck. It was nice knowing you. I do look good in black though."

He flounced back to the reception, just as Rebecca walked through the door.

"What's with the long face, Samara? Oh you were just born that way?" She dropped her bag at the side of the chair and switched her laptop on. "Things not going so well, sweetie? And I've had another successful day of matches. Looks like one of us is set for the top and the other is set for the dole queue."

"I have another business, remember? Plus, I'm confident that my first Aftercare clients will be together very soon."

"You have some clients? Who?" she asked.

Shit. I couldn't tell her about Jessica and Lachlan, and I definitely couldn't tell her about Holden and Julie-Ann.

"I'm saying nothing until the matches are in the bag." I turned to my desk and made sure there was nothing on screen or on my desk to give her any heads up should she come looking.

"Hope it's flame retardant, though I'll be ready and waiting for the meltdown." She smiled at me sweetly.

Yep, there was no way I was helping her to a promotion. It was definitely time for Rebecca to get what she deserved.

A one-way trip out of my life.

CHAPTER
13

Jessica

I was looking forward to some girly time outside of work. I'd dressed casually in jeans and a jumper and added a thick Winter coat. The lighthouse was in sight when I got a text.

Samara: I'm not coming today. I have bad sickness. So sorry. Have fun. Hope you see a familiar face that can keep you company instead.

My stomach sank. Great. No day out in the company of a friend after all. Instead, it would be another day by myself. Maybe I would head down to Jax's on my own after the lighthouse and introduce myself. I needed more friends.

"Hey, Jess."

I swivelled around quickly to find Lachlan standing behind me. The first thing I noticed was he was wearing a dark navy coat. I'd always loved that colour on him.

"Lachlan." I acknowledged. He carried on staring. "Well? Do you want something?"

His mouth narrowed, then he spoke. "Jess, I got your phone message about needing to talk. I agree, so I came to visit the lighthouse with you. I've been meaning to come anyway and find out some Withernsea history."

I placed a hand on my hip. "What are you talking about? What message? I've not sent you a message."

Lachlan tapped into his phone and turned it around to show me. There was a message sent from my phone. I checked the time it was sent, and all became clear.

"Samara. I've been set up. I'll kill her."

Lachlan's face clouded with disappointment. "You didn't send it?"

"No, an interfering Cupid rep did."

Realisation set in and he schooled his expression. "Got it. You don't want to talk after all." He began to walk away and then he turned back after a few steps. "I can visit another time. You go in."

I was about to nod and then I thought otherwise. We did need to be able to be civil to one another. We could start today. "No, it's fine. Let's go see what the view is like, shall we?"

He paused and then he nodded and turning back around we bought our tickets.

One hundred and forty-four steps took us to the top and to the view across Withernsea. It was fantastic but I could barely breathe by the time I got to the top, and Lachlan was the same.

"Some things have changed." He puffed. "We used to be able to climb to viewpoints without almost collapsing."

I laughed. "Yeah, I don't run anymore. I haven't for a long time."

"Me neither. Perhaps I need to start again. I could run along the beach front and the beach. Should be quite a workout."

"Yeah, it's a good idea." I turned back to the view.

"So how have you been, Jess? Really?"

I looked at him. "I'm okay. I love my work. The

jury's still out over whether my move to Withernsea was a good idea. There was nothing wrong with my previous job, but I fancied a change."

"Is the jury still out because of what my father did? Because I'm here."

I shook my head. "No, because I have to make new friends and it's not something that comes easily to me."

"I know."

We stared back out of the window, but rather than looking at the view, I could take a guess that we were both currently being transported back to the scene of our first meeting.

"This party is lame, isn't it?" I turned to see the most gorgeous man talking in my direction. Surely, he couldn't be speaking to me? I looked behind me. No one else was there.

"Sorry, am I interrupting? Are you looking for your date?" He asked, staring past me.

"No, no. I came alone. Well, I came with Amanda, a colleague, but she went off with a guy the minute we got here, so I'm not sure why I needed to be here. Looks like I was a Wingwoman."

"Ah, well I have a feeling that I'm the Wingman

seeing as my friend Ger disappeared with a blonde on arrival."

He held out a hand. "Lachlan."

I tried to surreptitiously wipe my palm on my trouser leg before shaking his hand. I was nervous and my hands always sweated profusely when I was nervous.

"Jessica."

"Well, Jessica. Seeing as we both have to wait for our friends to come back to tell us they're going to ditch us for the night and is that okay, where we will say yeah sure and not mean it; can I buy you a drink? Then when they do ditch us, we can have a good bitch about it behind their backs."

I smiled. "Okay."

A middle-aged man appeared behind us and he smiled at me. A big beaming smile. He had big cherubic cheeks and a pot belly. Weirdo. He mimed shooting an arrow and the weirdest thing happened. I actually felt a tingle and I felt an outpouring of love for the world for a moment. I saw Lachlan see my reaction and he quickly turned around.

"Excuse me." He said and he set off after the guy, who was trying to escape. I watched a terse exchange between the two and then Lachlan headed back.

"Everything okay?"

"Yeah. That was my father. He's so very nosy. Anyway, he's gone now, so how about I get you that drink?"

"Lachlan..."

"Don't worry, I'm not going to pester you with come ons. Just a drink between new friends, okay?"

"Well, I can't turn that down. I don't make friends easily."

"Really? A lovely woman like you?"

But I could feel the burning attraction between us and I knew we were going to be more than new friends.

I came around from my daze. Luckily, my eyes were still fixed out at the view. As I turned, I caught Lachlan staring at me. His arm moved and he picked up my hand.

My palm was sweating. Hurriedly, I pulled my arm away.

"Good, you're nervous. I am too." He looked into the distance as he spoke. I was aware that eye contact between us was difficult to hold. "I'm not going to pressure you over what happened, Jess. I know it was a lot to do with my work and I accept that. I've had a lot of years to reflect on what I'd been doing. At some point I really would like to chat about it all; but if it never happens, well, that will have to be okay. For now, could we try to be friends? I could do with a running buddy for starters." He patted a non-existent stomach. "Getting on a little now. It's harder to maintain."

"Maybe." I replied. But I doubted we could ever just be friends. We'd tried that before.

We lingered near the exit together, not knowing how to say goodbye.

"I was going to head to Jax's coffee shop. Her instant and filter coffee is amazing, but I thought I might try the real deal."

Lachlan's jaw dropped. "You've not been there yet? It's a must-do." He put his arm through mine. "Let's go. My treat."

I stiffened at the contact and he let me go. "Sorry. I get a bit excited about going to Jax's. It's been one of the best things about the move."

I shrugged. "Don't worry about it, but to apologise you're buying."

As we walked in to the welcoming Jax's with it's cute

little tables and bunting hung around, a small woman with a dark pixie crop came rushing over, a huge welcoming smile on her face.

"Hello, Sergeant Hart. Take a seat." She held out a hand, "and are you Jessica?"

"I am." I laughed politely, a little disconcerted. "Am I wearing a name badge I don't know about?"

She giggled. "No, Samara called me to say she thought I might see you today, although she'd taken a punt that it would be with you stomping in here in a temper asking for coffee and looking like you wanted to kill someone, namely her. I'm glad to see she got it wrong, although my coffee cures all ills."

"She's in big trouble." I said.

"Yeah, that's Sam's MO. She'll not care. Okay, menus are on the table, specials on the board behind the counter. Come up to the counter when you're ready to order."

"Thank you, Jax." Lachlan said. He pointed to a seat. "Over there, okay?"

"Sure."

I sat down, trying to gather my thoughts and emotions. I was sitting in a coffee shop with the ex-husband I still loved. What on earth was I doing? But he'd just told me he realised his mistakes and now I was feeling an emotion that had been missing in me for a long time. Hope. But I couldn't risk it. Couldn't bear to have my heart smashed to smithereens once more.

When Lachlan went up to the counter to order, a dark-haired woman sat in his seat.

"Oh, actually, someone is-"

"I know it's your husband's seat." The woman's cut-glass accent told me who she was before she introduced herself. Samara's friend, Ebony. A seer.

"It's good to meet you, Jessica. Samara speaks fondly of you. I'm Ebony. I'm a seer. I just had a vision, darling, and I need to pass it on to you. Now, sometimes things come to me very unclearly, but with you it's crystal, darling. Crystal clear."

"It is?"

"Yes. You have to tell your husband everything. Whether that's now or at a future point. You two are destined and will find no other love. So you either embark on choppy waters where things will get difficult and challenging; or you never swim again. It's your choice. Choose wisely." She got up and squeezed my shoulder, and then walked out of the coffee shop.

Lachlan brought my drink over to the table. "Our toasties will be about ten minutes."

I nodded and went to pick up my cup. It

wobbled in my hand and spilled on the table. I couldn't do this, not right now. Not with all these feelings of pressure I was experiencing. I had to get away.

"I remembered something. Sorry, Lachlan. I have to go. Excuse me." I pushed my chair back, the sound of it scraping against the floor making other customers turn around. Their gazes made me want to escape even quicker, my heart thudded in my chest.

"Jess? Jess, what's the matter? Are you okay?"

"I'll be fine. Please, just leave me be, Lachlan. I need some time okay? Time to think."

He stepped back and stood straight and formal. The policeman stood in front of me now. "Yes, of course. Okay, Jessica. Thank you for letting me accompany you on the lighthouse visit. Take care."

I dashed out of the coffee shop and headed straight for Jetty's.

I was hungry. The smell of cooking at Jax's had been heavenly, but I needed space from Lachlan. I also felt a need to rebel against what Ebony had said; about Lachlan and me being destined. I sat down at the table and waited for the waiter to come over.

"What can I get you?" He said as surly as ever. Could I really do this?

I saw Max hovering near the doorway, and I beckoned him in.

"Oh, he's been hovering there for half the morning." Waiter man said. "Strange dude."

"Max is lovely, just unusual. He just needs to find a boyfriend to keep him occupied." I stated. I took a deep breath. "Anyway, could I have a waffle with ice cream and chocolate sauce; a hot chocolate; and your phone number by any chance?"

"My phone number?" Waiter man looked shocked.

"Yes, I wondered if you fancied a date?" I asked him. "Oh and knowing your name would be good too." Max was on his way over, so I signalled for him to give me a minute.

"Is he just really shy?" The waiter said.

"No, he'll be totally overexcited in a minute when he hears about the date. Oh." I stuttered. "That's if there is one of course."

"Oh, yes. Totally, I'll go out on a date. My name is Brandon. Brandon Walsh. Let me write my details here. Now I must go or Jetty will be on my case, but maybe The Marine at eight tomorrow evening? It's my day off."

"Sure. It's a date." I told him, and he went to process my order while Max bounded over.

"Sorry about that." I told him. "Only I was just arranging a date with Brandon."

Max's jaw dropped. "What? Brandon, behind the counter, Brandon?"

"Yes. I'm meeting him at The Marine at 8pm tomorrow."

Max slumped in his seat. "Well knock me down with a feather. I was sure he batted for my team."

"Sorry, bro." I smiled smugly. I couldn't help it. I'd got up the courage to ask someone out and they'd said yes!

"Oh, plenty more arseholes in Withernsea, I'm sure." He winked.

"What makes you think Brandon is an arseho— Oh, you were being very rude."

Max guffawed.

"Hope it's not our date making you hysterical." Brandon said bringing my hot chocolate.

"No, just my own wit." Max said.

"Are you wanting to order anything?"

"Jessica, will you order for me." Max once again slumped in his seat. "Only my processes are way off. Both professionally and personally I just can't seem to get my point across right now."

"Well there's always tomorrow." Brandon said. "So what does he want, erm?"

"Jessica." I said. "My name's Jessica."

God, I hope the date went smoother than our introductions.

CHAPTER 14

Samara

I'd expected a call from Jess with her screaming down the line at me, but there was nothing. I started to get excited that things might be going to plan, especially when Jax texted to tell me that Jess and Lachlan had come into the cafe together and ordered lunch. But then she texted again to say Jess had left without eating.

My phone buzzed once more.

Max: Your Aftercare Cupiding is fucked. Jess just arranged a date with the waiter from Jetty's.

. . .

I quickly typed back.

Samara: You've seen her? What happened with Lachlan?

Max: We're in Jetty's having waffles and hot chocolate. I've not asked. Why should I find out and get aggro? You engineered this whole thing; you should suffer the consequences.

Samara: Max!

Max: Okay, okay. I want a horse and carriage to transport my coffin you hear?

I waited a few minutes and then my phone buzzed again.

. . .

Max: They went to the lighthouse, had lunch ordered, then Ebony said something to her about Lachlan being her future and she wigged out.

Samara: FFS. Okay. Thank you.

Max: PS she said to tell you that you're so dead on Monday.

Huh, Monday seemed a long way off. With Jessica and Lachlan's get together in complete disarray, I needed to make sure tonight's couple had no such interruptions or distractions.

"Johnny, babes."

"Yes, love?"

"Will you come to The Marine with me tonight? I've a matchmake to organise. It'd be good to have you there. If it all goes wrong, you can get drunk on my behalf."

"Sounds like an offer I can't refuse."

"Yep, you can't, but I asked nicely."

. . .

We arrived at The Marine thirty minutes before Julie-Ann and Holden were due to arrive. I was surprised therefore to find Julie-Ann at one table and Holden at the next one. Did they look so different they wouldn't recognise each other? I sent Johnny to the bar as both of the others were already nursing a drink each: Julie-Ann a very large glass of red and Holden a pint of beer. I hugged Julianne and told her I'd be just a minute and then I went to talk to Holden. I wanted to double check it was definitely him. As I got near him he moved backwards.

"Erm, Mr. Bisley? I'm Samara Leighton. We spoke on the phone?"

"I'm not sure it's a good idea we meet now." His eyes flicked around the place as if looking for where he could run to.

I looked over at Julie-Ann shrugging my shoulders, but she was also looking at me with a similar perplexed expression. I started to feel my face.

"Do I look weird to you? Do I have something on my face?" I asked Holden.

"You look weird in that you keep talking to someone at the next table when there's no one there." He declared.

"What do you mean no one there? Julie-Ann is at the next table."

"No, no she isn't." He tried edging around the table.

I put my arm up. "Okay, just suspend your belief that I'm completely cuckoo for a moment and hear me out. When you look at the table next to you, what do you see?"

"An empty table."

"If I promise to sit with my husband at the empty table can you just stay here for like an extra half an hour? Finish your pint, and just give me some extra time. Only I don't know if you're aware of the strange happenings in Withernsea, but it would seem there's a, let's call it, a 'problem' with you and Julie-Ann getting together and I can sort it out."

Holden made a bolt for it, so I tripped him up and sat on top of his back.

"Don't try and buck me off, I'm a pregnant lady. We wouldn't want me injured."

Johnny came running over. "Samara, what the hell are you doing?" He lifted me off Holden, who looked up at him, anger blazing on his face.

"Can you keep your wife away from me? She's been riding the train to Crazyland. No doubt a friend of Rebecca's, aren't you?"

Julie-Ann came running over. "Why are you two acting so crazy? I thought I was meeting Holden?"

"You can't see each other. There must be a spell." I took my phone out while still not letting Holden get past me. "Shelley! Whizz to The Marine, I have an emergency situation." I put the phone down.

"STAND STILL BOTH OF YOU." I yelled. "Please, give me a few minutes then you can leave."

"I'm phoning the police, this is preposterous." Holden said. Then the curtain behind him breezed and Shelley stood there.

"Where the hell have you come from? Maybe it's me. Maybe I'm the crazy one." Holden began tapping his head.

"Shelley. These two can't see each other. Can you check for spells please and quickly?"

Shelley said some words of a spell and a white cobweb-like string wrapped round them both. "Right, first, let's calm them down. Don't worry, no one else can see this but you, Johnny, and these two." I watched as the couple visibly relaxed. Then they became completely covered in what looked like a white bodysuit that cracked and fell away disappearing as it hit the floor.

"Holden?" Julie-Ann said.

"Julie-Ann." Holden said.

"Thank absolute fuck." I said.

"Right, just in case anyone saw anything they shouldn't." Shelley raised a brow, then using her part-vampire skills she addressed the room and used her power of suggestion to make them think they'd seen nothing strange here tonight. Johnny returned to the bar and ordered another beer, and wine for the couple.

"I'm so sorry, I honestly thought you were a complete mental case." Holden said.

"It's fine. Totally understandable if it looked to each of you like I was talking to myself." I giggled. "It's quite funny when you think of it."

"I didn't think it was the slightest bit funny, Samara. You could have got hurt." Johnny was not amused.

"Well, thank you for taking this spell thing off us." Holden said. "Who'd have thought some magic was real? But why did you not do the suggestion spell on us?"

"You said Rebecca stalked you. It's not fair to wipe your mind right now while I investigate further. I will raise the issue with Cupid Inc, but until then you need to be able to be aware of her. After that we will come and wipe away any memories of us and magic though. We'll just leave you believing you met by accident here in The Marine."

They nodded but I could tell they were both disappointed that it would happen.

"So we've lived less than an hour away from each other all these years and never knew. That bitch has a lot to answer for." Julie-Ann spat out.

"Let's not waste another moment of our time. Come on, let me take you on a date, for a meal and," he dropped to one knee. "Will you marry me, Julie-Ann?"

"Yes." She gasped. "Oh my, yes. Yes, I will."

It was then that I realised—and I couldn't believe it had taken me so long—that the single tingles I was feeling from them both were very strong still. I'd believed it was because they should have been together and had been kept apart for so long. But it wasn't. It was because, and I sent my Cupid senses out once more to double and triple check. Yep. No arrows had been fired at them in the first place. Rebecca had not pointed and shot at them at all.

As realisation dawned, the door burst open and the lady herself came hurtling through.

"How fucking dare you?" She screeched. "Once again you're trying to ruin my life. Do not fire those arrows at him. You hear me? Not until his single tingles come for me. Then you can fire them."

"It's been years, Rebecca. When are you going to give this up?" Holden sighed. "I can't live my life. I always have one eye open searching for her. She just won't leave me alone."

I was actually at a loss for what to do. And then I thought about it a little. Why should I think what to do? Let the queen of chaos do it herself.

"FATE!" I shouted.

A boom appeared and then there she was, but then there was another bang and a guy appeared. He was tall and reed thin and his hair was blue at one side and black at the other. He and Fate looked quite alike.

"What have you done?" she yelled at the guy.

He shrugged his shoulders smirking. "Why should you always have everything your own way? I thought we'd take a chance, so I 'helped' Rebecca find them."

"They were fated to get together tonight and live happily ever after." She yelled again.

He shrugged his shoulders once more.

"Anyone know what's happening?" I asked a sea of agog faces.

The guy looked at me and at the others. "Oh, my apologies. Allow me to introduce myself. I'm Fate's brother, Chance. I thought we should mix things up a little."

"I'm so sorry." Fate turned to us. "He does this occasionally, and no one can actually stop him. So on this occasion there's nothing I can do. What will be will be."

She grabbed his arm and they both disappeared to wherever they came from.

It was while we were all taken aback and standing around stunned that Julie-Anne ran up to Rebecca and threw a punch that knocked her clean out.

"Well if no one else can do anything then this little human will sort it out. Keep away from my man, bitch."

She had a point.

I called Cupid. Rebecca was his mess ultimately and he should decide how to deal with her.

While she was out cold, I summoned my bow and arrows. "Let's get this union created once and for all." I told them, and I shot them both.

I watched as love filled them both up. There was

no space to hate Rebecca any longer within them. Their souls had bound together. We wished them goodnight and all the best for their future.

Then we waited for Cupid to turn up with the clean up crew.

CHAPTER 15

Samara

We were supposed to be off on a Sunday. Instead it was ten am and we were all sat in Cupid Inc's reception.

Cupid's voice boomed out. "Our first week has proved very interesting."

That was one way of putting it.

"So, Samara, very well done on your Aftercare project. We have one set of happy customers." He paused and then looked at Jessica briefly and then back to me. "Now for another." He turned to Jessica. "I hear you have a date tonight, my lovely."

"Yes," Jessica smiled smugly at him.

His face paled which was never a good sign in a rosy cheeked Cupid. "Well, moving swiftly on. How are you progressing with Maisie, Max?"

"A solid first week's work. Jess is doing some counselling work with us to try to get to the bottom of why Maisie can't find a partner."

"And what have you uncovered?"

"That she's undateable, so we know for a fact now that she's in the right department. Like I said, solid first week. Firstly, make sure they are genuinely undateable."

"Well, we'll see what further revelations you unearth on week two. And no, you can't suggest having her put down."

"Hahahahaha. As if I'd do that." Max said, picking up his pad and crossing something off of it. He caught me staring at him. "What? It was an option. Leave no stone unturned."

"So now I must address the elephant in the room." Cupid said.

"Actually, she's not in the room now." Max guffawed. "Sorry."

Cupid sighed.

"As Max may have told you, Rebecca has been admitted to a place of respite."

"Where all the nutters go." Max added helpfully.

"She'll have some therapy, but ultimately when a

Cupid goes wayward there's only one thing you can do."

Max picked his pad back up. "Can I have my sister put to sleep?"

"Enough." Cupid commanded and Max paled and sat still.

"My apologies, Sir."

"Rebecca will be stripped of any memories of Cupid Inc whatsoever. Your parents have signed a consent form that they will follow our direct orders. We will make up a new life for her. Rebecca will believe that she has always lived in Australia and to that end her and your parents as you know will be emigrating."

Max was fighting to keep his mouth closed.

"Carry on the good work. A new point and shooter for the area will be appointed in due course, but I've decided to keep that part of things entirely separate from this business. Instead I will appoint a receptionist so you may be free to work without interruption."

With that Cupid bade us farewell and left.

Max let out a huge exhale. "I got rid of my sister and my parents. We need to throw a huge party to celebrate. Who's coming to the pub?"

"I have a date tonight." Jess reminded him.

"I'm pregnant and can't drink. Plus, I think I had enough excitement for one night, last night in that place. Thank goodness we know people who can wipe memories."

"Hopefully my night will be a lot calmer." Jessica said. "Anyway, if that's all, I'm going to go back to my flat to start primping and preening for tonight."

When she'd left, I went over and hugged Max. "Are you really so excited to see them all gone?"

"I really am. I love my parents, but I'll love them more if they're on another continent, and well, I can't stand my sister. Sorry, you can't choose biological family. Well, maybe you can, I don't know where we're up to with cloning and genetic selection, but she's gone and good riddance to her. The bitch has left the building."

"Maybe she's going to be really nice now that she's got her mind wiped?" I suggested.

"Yeah, and maybe Jessica's date is going to be a huge success." He rolled his eyes.

"Why wouldn't it be?"

"Because I'm telling you, that guy is gay. No one is more surprised than me that he accepted her offer of a date, because that guy has been giving me goo-goo eyes all last week. He must not be out of the closet. Anyway, it's going to be a complete disaster. I just know it."

"In that case then maybe we should hang around tonight, nearby?" I suggested, while internally my mind was screaming 'don't do it'.

"I was so hoping you'd say that." Max grinned. "And I'll wear my best clothes just in case I'm right, so waiterboy and I can ride off into the sunset together."

"Er, wouldn't you want to console Jess instead?"

He pulled a face looking around. "Why do you think you're coming too, sweetiepie?"

One day I'd lose it and strangle him with his own feather boa.

CHAPTER 16

Jessica

I had eight missed calls from Lachlan and four texts all asking me to contact him. The last text had said he wouldn't text me any further, but he really would like to meet with me again to talk, or if I liked, to simply go for a run.

I should have been excited for my date but instead I wished I'd never even arranged it. There was no future for myself and Brandon, and really it wasn't fair to have asked him on a date, not when I knew my heart belonged to Lachlan and always would. I figured the least I could do was turn up, have a drink, and ask Brandon if he wanted to be friends. Feeling that was the best plan, rather than primp and preen myself, I watched old movies all afternoon and then half an hour before my date I put on some light make-up, jeans and a sweater and I headed to The Marine.

When I arrived, I spotted Brandon sitting at a table near the window. Rather than look pleased to see me, he looked past me as if he was looking for someone else. Then his face fell, before a look of resignation came over him, and he stood up and gave me a quick hug.

"No date then?"

Jesus. How did he know just by looking at me that I wasn't interested in that way? Maybe it was my low-key appearance that gave it off?

"No, sorry. But I thought maybe we could be friends?"

Brandon nodded. "That'd be cool. Would you like a drink?"

Wow. This had gone so much easier than I had imagined.

"Yes, I'll have a glass of white wine please."

"Okay, I'll be right back."

I sat back in my seat feeling relaxed. We were just going to be friends and now I could enjoy a nice relaxing drink with a new pal. All the pressure was off. I sighed. Maybe I didn't know what to do about Lachlan, but for tonight I might just allow myself to get a little bit merry and maybe I could see if Brandon had unrequited love or was undate-able. If so, I'd do my best to help my new friend find a date.

Brandon had just brought my drink over to me and sat back down when suddenly he jumped a foot in the air. "Oh my god, he's here. He's here. I thought he couldn't make it? Fuck. How do I look, Jessica?"

I span around to see Max and Samara heading over to us. She beckoned me over and confused, I walked towards her while Max took my place at the table. He even started drinking my wine!

"What's going on? Why are you here?"

"Max is convinced your date is gay."

I laughed. "If that was the case then why did he agree to go on a date with me?"

Samara shrugged her shoulders. "Damned if I know, so let's get a drink and go and join them for five and see if we can find out what's going on."

As we went over with our drinks a loud cackle emitted from Max's mouth.

"Oh my god, your gob is so big." Samara looked around the pub.

"I know right, and what I can fit in it is impres-sive." He winked at Brandon who went bright red.

"What's so funny anyway?" I asked.

"Oh, honey. Somehow you two got your wires

crossed. Brandon thought you were arranging a date for him with me."

"No, it was clear the date was for both of us."

Brandon shook his head.

I replayed our conversation the best I could remember. Max had turned up while I was arranging it and I remember saying he'd be excited about the date. It was entirely possible we'd got our wires crossed.

Well then, I was free of 'arranging a panic date' guilt and had actually made my own first match. I might not have a bow and arrows, but I certainly had the talent. However, I decided I'd quit while I was ahead and stick with psychology.

"You don't look very disappointed that your date went wrong." Samara queried.

"I'm really not. There was no future for me and Brandon."

"That's right, there really wasn't. Single tingles." She said and producing a bow and arrow she shot through Brandon and Max.

"So have you finally realised you should be with Lachlan and there's no fighting your ideal match?"

"Maybe." I smiled at her. "I think I'll send him a text to see if he wants to go for a run sometime, and then take it from there."

"At least you'd be running with him, not away from him; but you need to tell him the truth. He deserves to know. Otherwise it will always be there eating away at you."

"Yeah, I know you're right." I sighed.

"I know that if I lost my baby when Johnny was away, I'd have wanted him to know so that we could grieve together. You shouldn't have had to shoulder that burden on your own."

"You're right. Do you want another water?" I asked her.

"Oh why not, let's push the boat out and put me a slice of lemon in it this time."

I went to the bar and that's when it all went wrong.

A fight broke out near to where I'd just been standing and I watched in horror as Samara was pushed out of the way by one of the men, lost her footing, and fell straight into a table, the corner hitting her in the stomach.

"Samara!" I screamed, running back towards her. She was lying on the floor clutching her stomach, her eyes filled with panic. Max phoned the police and an ambulance, and I phoned Johnny. The fight had been taken outside and I could still see punches being thrown through the window, but right now my concern was for my friend and her baby.

"What's happening? Are you bleeding?" I asked her.

"I don't know. I can't feel anything, but my stomach hurts so bad. Oh God, my baby."

"Baby!" Max gasped. "You're having a baby?"

"Yes, I didn't want to tell anyone until I was past twelve weeks."

"Oh, of course, I get that." He went down to the floor and sat behind her. "Breathe carefully, darling. Lean back on me and clutch my hand. If you get any pain feel free to squeeze my hand."

"She's not in labour, Max."

"I don't know what to do with injured pregnant women!" Max shouted.

"I'm feeling a lot better now. I think I just got a bit winded." Samara said, trying to stand up. We wouldn't let her move.

"You're to stay still and resting, honey, until you've been checked over." A paramedic came through the door and Max's eyes widened.

"Can we say I got injured and need checking over too?"

"I've got a paramedic dress up outfit at home, I can give you a thorough work-up." Brandon said.

Then the police followed through the door and suddenly I was faced with Lachlan once more.

Johnny arrived. He'd phoned Theo who'd whizzed him to the pub. He looked sick to his stomach from the journey and I bet he'd give his wife even more sympathy for her morning sickness from now on. He accompanied Samara into the ambulance and then they were off. Lachlan and his colleagues had apprehended most of the drunks involved in the fight. There was just one who'd got away.

"Hopefully, one of his enemies will grass his name and address to us and we can pick him up later." Lachlan said. "Anyway, come on, let me see you home."

"But you're working."

"I've told them my ex-wife is involved and that I'm making sure you're home and safe. I have time owing. They're more than capable of booking a few drunks. Let's go." He told me. I followed him out of the pub.

Lachlan took my keys off me and opened the

door at the bottom of the stairwell and then he walked up the stairs and opened the next door.

"Alarm code?" He asked.

I told him and he turned the alarm off, before turning to help me out of my coat. "Lachlan, I'm not an invalid. I only witnessed the events. No one hurt me."

"Yeah, but if they had." His eyes showed concern as I stood in front of him, and then they showed hunger. The next moment his lips were on mine.

I didn't want to, but I pushed him away.

"Lachlan, I-"

"I'm sorry. I'd better leave." He told me, turning for the door. I grabbed his arm. "No. You don't understand. I wanted to, but we need to talk first. There's something I have to tell you, from before."

I beckoned over to the sofa and I fixed us a glass of wine each and then I confessed about the baby.

"You lost our baby and you never said a word? What were you thinking?" Lachlan spat. His eyes were full of fury and he leapt to his feet. "You were pregnant, you lost it, and your response to that was to leave me?"

"You were always at work."

"Do you really think I'd have gone to work if I'd have known you'd lost our baby? What kind of monster do you take me for? I might have overlooked you and taken you for granted while I tried to secure the promotion to better our life, but I was doing that because I loved you. However misguided my attempts were, I did it for us." He paced around.

"I am so sorry. I know what I did was wrong, but I didn't see why both of us should suffer if our marriage was coming to an end anyway. I thought if I left then you could concentrate on the job."

"My life is nothing without you in it. Don't you understand that? I loved you. I still love you. But I can't be here right now, Jess. I don't know what to think and what to do. I need some time."

He made for the exit, but just as he reached it an almighty crash came and glass exploded from the now broken window. The brick and the fragments stopped about an inch from my body. I was surprised my shriek didn't break the rest of the windows. Before I knew what was happening, Lachlan had picked me up and was walking me out of the apartment.

"What are you doing?"

"I'm taking you home. To my home. And we're going to talk about things, Jessica. Properly talk about things. With a counsellor; you must know some with your profession. And we're going to move past all this and then we're going to get remarried and have children, and if you want you can be the career woman and I'll stay home because you are mine, and I am yours, and that's final. Do you understand, Miss Fazakerley?"

I was dumbstruck, but boy was he hot when he was masterful. I just nodded my head before resting it on his shoulders. He carried me out of the building 'Officer and a Gentleman' style and inside I swooned.

CHAPTER 17

Cupid

It'd almost gone wrong once more, but I'd known Jessica's confession would cause problems between them. Fate had told me so. But I was Cupid and if anyone could sort the two of them, it was me. Samara had managed to get another undateable matched tonight—Max—and so as far as I was concerned, she'd definitely passed her probation period.

So I decided to take matters into my own hands once more. The first brick had brought Lachlan to Jessica's door, the second had stopped him from leaving without her. And even better for me, one of those middle-aged men who'd been fighting in the pub happened to be passing, so as I threw the brick through the window, a chasing policeman had accused him of it, carting him off to the local station.

A brick through the window, just far enough to cause a fright, but not too much that it would cause an injury. Of course, I'm Cupid, a perfect shot.

And I hoped soon, I'd get to be a perfect grandad.

CHAPTER 18

Samara

They'd done checks and a scan on me. I had a picture of our little baby. Johnny had told me straight that any matchmaking took place in working hours in the office and that I was going nowhere near bars any more unless he was there to protect me. I was more than happy to stay home with my little family from now on.

It was funny. My parents were the worst parents in the world. They'd never given a damn about me and never would, and I'd carried a lot of baggage around about that fact. But now me and Johnny were going to be parents, I realised that none of that mattered any more. It was the future that mattered, and the future was me, Johnny, and our baby. I also had the most incredible job at Cupid Inc and my grooming business. Cupid had called to see me as soon as I got home and brought the most enormous bunch of red roses with him, along with an employment contract. I'd matched up two couples and he was hopeful we'd have a third soon as he told me about his brick trick to get the Harts reunited.

And when he said that, I had the most amazing idea. Cupid Inc to me would always be the name of the main branch. I felt we needed our new business to have a fresh name of its own, because it would soon be being rolled out across the country. Cupid loved it. We'd be having a new name put up soon above the door.

HEARTS REUNITED

Jessica was at work, but she'd phoned to say she'd pop in tomorrow to visit. That she knew Max was coming after work tonight and she felt I'd be exhausted after that. I'd already had Mabel here for most of the day. She'd put in a day's annual leave at work when she'd heard, bless her, and she'd fussed round me and insisted Johnny go to work when an emergency came in. I had a feeling that I had a new mother figure in my life anyway now in Mabel, and that was fine with me.

Max entered the bedroom. "Girlfriend, do you know how much you have aged me with the stress? I had to pop out at lunch for highlights to cover the grey. I'm sending you the bill."

I rolled my eyes at him.

"Obviously, I'm only joking. I went into Jetty's at lunchtime and got down and dirty with Brandon in the staff bathroom."

I placed my head in my hands. "What a visual."

"Do you know. I think I'll marry that boy. I do. When you know you know, it's true."

"I hit you with arrows, mate. He's your one." I told him.

"I thought I'd felt extra warm and fuzzy. But you know me, I'm like that anyway, so I couldn't be sure." He clapped his hands.

"Oh I'm going to look at diamonds. For me of course. Make sure you hint to him what I want. And by hint, I mean tell him directly."

I rolled my eyes.

"Anyway, how are you? How is my niece or nephew?"

"I'm fine, and excuse me?"

"I'm Uncle Max, its non-negotiable, darling, so accept it."

I passed him my scan picture. "Here's your niece or nephew, Uncle Max."

He looked at the photo and a tear fell from his eye.

"Samara, I know we've not known each other that long, but seriously, in that short time you've been more of a sister to me than that bitch who biologically was ever had been. I love you and I swear I will love and protect this baby. I'll babysit and everything. I'll even accept the possibility of baby sick or poop on my designer threads. That's how much love I have in me for you."

"Come here, you big softie." I said and I gave him the biggest hug. "You can be my honorary brother no problem. The more family me and my baby have around us the better. I'd be honoured."

"Do uncles get push-presents?" He said hopefully.

I let go of him. "No they bloody don't. When I push a huge baby out of my hoo-hah it will be all about me, you hear?"

"Not about the baby, then? Just all about you?" He winked.

We laughed because we knew that once my

bubba was here it would definitely all be about the baby.

"Anyway, I'm sorry that I've passed my probation while you still need to get Maisie a date." I looked at him sympathetically, only to be met with a smirk.

"You didn't? Did you actually get her a date?"

"Yup. Totally accidentally, but ssshhh." He put a finger to his lips. "She'd been in this morning bugging me and being a right pain in the arse and not in a nice way. So when she left I followed her and as soon as she became a cat I shoved her in a basket and took her to your grooming salon. Cats hate being wet, right? I told India that my cat loved a bath and she needed the works."

"You evil swine."

"I figured when she'd endured a wash and blow dry and I collected her, that I'd only have to threaten it again and that would be enough to get her in line."

"Then what happened?"

"Well it would appear that she changed in the middle of the wash session and revealed all her naked glory to India. Who kissed a girl and liked it. They're together and the tingles were strong when I went to collect her. Maisie declared me a genius for thinking outside of the box. Basically, I'd not been thinking about a box at all, when all along someone with one was her perfect match. And with that there will be no more talk of pussy or pussies for as long as is possible." He shuddered.

"So did you shoot them?"

"I did and then Cupid called in and congratulated me. He said he and Shelley had deliberately picked the most difficult client because they knew that if I could make a match for her, I could match any undateable."

"And now we are Cupids again. Fully-fledged Cupids. Did you hear about our new name?"

"I did. I love it. Hearts Reunited, and Cupid is very smug that Lachlan and Jessica plan to work things out."

"God, I love a happy ever after." I hugged Max.

"Me too, sister. Me too."

EPILOGUE

Samara

August

My daughter let out a wail of protest as I passed her to her Auntie Jessica, but only for a moment and then her green eyes closed again.

"Oh my, she's so very beautiful." Jessica cooed.

"Well, you'll have your own soon." I smiled. Jess was three months pregnant and her and Lachlan had remarried four months ago.

"Yes, Cupid is getting my maternity leave covered. He pretended to moan about it, but we know really he's smug that we're together again."

"Just think." Max piped up from the chair opposite us. "Just a few months ago we were all single and now we're all engaged or married." He held up his hand. Max was never one to pass up an opportunity to show off his huge sparkler, or the flashy diamond on his finger.

Rosa Maxine Leighton chose that moment to fill her nappy and was swiftly passed to her daddy, who loved her so damn much he could hardly put her down.

"Have you got a full day of visitors then?" Johnny and I had said no visitors other than his family for the first week, though Mabel, my now-cemented-into-my-life mother figure had been included. She was never far away with a fresh pack of nappies or some extra bibs.

"Yes, Shelley will be over in an hour. She's bringing three-week-old Leo who she says will no doubt be Rosa's protector."

"So many babies. What with Ebony pregnant too and Kim's triplets. It's like a whole new generation for Withernsea."

"Yes, and even though I'm thoroughly knackered and sore, I know I want Johnny to give me at least two more babies. I want a huge family if we're lucky."

"So what about the fact that Rosa will be a Cupid? Does that still bother you? The genetics research is yet to uncover anything to stop the familial gene."

"I don't mind at all now we have Hearts Reunited. Our children can take over from us, can't they?"

My phone beeped and picking it up my forehead tensed at the message.

Mum: We heard you had a daughter, so I suppose congratulations are in order.

That was it. No asking to see her. Her words were yet another disappointment in a long line of them. I swiftly blocked her number and did the same with my father's and then I placed the phone back in my bag as Johnny returned with my daughter who smelled delicious and would be told every day just how much I loved her.

The truth was I had all my family right here, in Withernsea.

THE END

A new paranormal romantic comedy will be out later in the year. To receive updates, sign up to my newsletter:

www.subscribepage.com/f8v2u5

ABOUT ANDIE

Andie M. Long is author of *Amazon Number One Erotic Thrillers* **Saviour,** and **The Alphabet Game** amongst others. She lives in Sheffield with her son and long suffering partner. When not being partner, mother, employee or writer she can usually be found on Facebook or walking her whippet, Bella.

Andie's Reader Hangout
(not a street team, just a place to hang and have fun)

Mailing List
(get a free ebook of DATING SUCKS on sign-up)

EMAIL
contact@andiemlongwriter.com

ALSO BY ANDIE

VISIT ANDIE'S AMAZON PAGE FOR ALL TITLES
AND FOLLOW FOR RELEASE AND SALE
UPDATES:

www.amazon.co.uk/Andie-M-Long/e/B00HP5D2NK

PARANORMAL ROMANTIC COMEDY

SUPERNATURAL DATING AGENCY

The Vampire wants a Wife

A Devil of a Date

Hate, Date, or Mate

Here for the Seer

Didn't Sea it Coming

Phwoar and Peace

CUPID INC

Crazy, Stupid, Lazy, Cupid

Cupid and Psych

PARANORMAL REVERSE HAREM

FILTHY R$CH

Filthy R$ch Vampire Playboys

Filthy R$ch Vampire Husbands

NEW ADULT PARANORMAL ROMANCE

SISTERS OF ANDLUSAN

Last Rites

First Rules

CONTEMPORARY ROMANCE

THE ALPHA SERIES

The Alphabet Game

The Alphabet Wedding

The Calendar Game

The Baby Game

Box set of books 1-3 available

The Alphabet Game: Play It Playbook

THE BALL GAMES SERIES

Balls

Snow Balls

New Balls Please

Balls Fore

Jingle Balls

Curve Balls

Birthing Balls

Upcoming: Balls Up

The Ball Games Bundle – books 1-4 is available

STANDALONE SUSPENSE TITLES

Underneath

Saviour

Mine

WOMEN'S FICTION

Journey to the Centre of Myself

ROMANTIC COMEDY CO-WRITES

The Bunk Up - co-written with DH Sidebottom

Road Trip – co-written with Laura Barnard

WRITING AS ANGEL DEVLIN

www.amazon.com/author/angeldevlin

Contemporary steamy romance. Click the link for available titles.

CPSIA information can be obtained
at www.ICGtesting.com
Printed in the USA
BVHW030821040619
550101BV00001B/18/P

9 781096 755401